Virago

'Endgame'

Deb Mills-Burns

1

ISBN: 9798851336355

Prologue

I entered the orphanage and was met with the same steely-eyed look I'd encountered in the last three orphanages I'd stayed in; it was a warning I knew all too well and usually followed with 'behave yourself here, young lady, you won't get many more chances to find a family who will want you with your current behaviour.' At just eight years old, I'd spent most of my life in care. I'd already been to two families, but they couldn't handle my behaviour. I only wanted to feel love, but the anger overwhelmed all my emotions, and I knew I had to be a survivor. I couldn't show any weakness; there were too many predators, both adults and children.

I was shown to a room that contained eight beds; a group of four girls around my age glared at me as I walked through the door. I responded with a one-fingered salute to let them know I wasn't scared of them; they turned their heads and carried on with whatever they were doing. The carer who had brought me in grabbed my arm and said sternly, 'Remember what I said; there won't be many more chances for you, young lady.' She got the bird, too.' As she shook her head and muttered on her way out of the room, I noticed an olive-skinned girl looking across, giggling as I caught her eye; she stuck her middle finger up at me; I laughed back and then quickly tried to redeem my 'don't give a fuck' cover, but it was too late, I'd felt that fluttery feeling you get when you like someone, I didn't even know what it meant at the time, but now at the ripe old age of thirty-eight it's the feeling every lesbian gets when they meet their soulmate.

My best childhood memories are filled with the following six weeks of my life, aged eight years old and making what I thought at the time was a best friend. Jane was so kind and loving; her impact on me in those six weeks turned me into a child who might have had a chance. My behaviour improved as I couldn't bear to be sent away again and leave Jane behind. I wanted her in my life forever because the anger started to subside. I began feeling warm and fuzzy and felt someone cared for me for the first time. I should have realised sooner that someone as good and honest as Jane was never going to stick around with me, and when a man and woman came to visit Jane, and she spent time away with them each week, I should have known that she was going to go to her forever family. The day she walked out of the orphanage, I felt like a knife had been driven into my heart; as she got into the car, she looked up at me, blew me a kiss, and then stuck her finger up at me, and that was it I had lost my only chance to love.

Only a short time after Jane left, Ritchie came to the home. He was a male version of me, with his 'I don't give a fuck attitude,' and between the pair of us, we terrorised the carers and became the 'top dogs' of the home; Ritchie had never found his forever family either, and the pair of us bounced from home to home, until one day a kind-faced lady and a stern-faced man came and took us both.

By the time I was seventeen years old, Bette and Dave had turned the pair of us into decent kids, and we both joined the Army inspired by Dave's stories of his service in the Special Air Service.

Ritchie joined the Marines, and I joined the Intelligence Corps, and we eventually ended up in the same barracks for deployment to Northern Ireland in 1998 and Iraq in 2003. He was more than just a brother in arms; he guided me through my darkest days and kept me on the straight and narrow. After losing Jane, nothing seemed worth living for, and I spiralled continuously; it was always Ritchie who brought me back, and he always tried to keep me going and gave me regular Close Protection and investigation jobs, paying me well and allowing me to keep going with life.

This job, though, would change everything.

'I've got an easy gig for you, Ginny,' Ritchie said, 'good pay, few months in Dubai, all expenses paid, looking after a rich bitch who also isn't too bad on the eye and wait for the best bit rumour is 'she's a raving lezza like you, so you might even get ya fingers wet if you're lucky,' here you go, I've done a draft op order, cast your eyes on that' Ritchie had such a way with words.

As I read through the op order, I went through the fine details of the 'target.'

Ellen Fatima Shervani, aged forty years old, an Irish/Iranian businesswoman, has several properties: one in Kensington, London, an inherited family estate in Killiney, County Dublin, and an estate in Jumeirah, Dubai, where she is currently residing for a six-month visit to see her father, Amir Shervani.

A six-month all-expenses trip to Dubai while earning a shit load of cash would appeal to anybody in the game, and gigs like this are sporadic. However, I hated Dubai; being in a country that treats homosexuality as a punishable crime is never a good move for a lesbian whose most recent favourite pastime is getting shitfaced and sleeping with random women. So, as lucrative as the job was, I wasn't that interested until I flicked over the page, and there she was in a striking picture: Elle Shervani, one of the most beautiful women I had ever set eyes on; she had the perfect genes of the Irish and Iranian/ Persians, olive-skinned with dark hair and the most piercing blue eyes I have ever seen. Ritchie laughed and said there it is, hook, line, and sinker,' the temptation to get ya tongue in between those fine legs is too much to say no. 'Shut up, you tit Ritchie, can't you just tame it down? You know the biggest rule to never break is to sleep with a client; add another coffee and a cheese and ham toastie to this order, and I might think about it.

Chapter 1 – Happy anniversary

I woke up to the early summer sun shining through the blinds; I must get blackout curtains, I thought. I turned to face my beautiful wife-to-be; she was still dreaming away. Her olive-skinned face looked so peaceful, and her natural beauty shone as brightly as the sun.

Today would be the last time in a while waking up next to her beauty, as she was briefly returning to Afghanistan for four weeks to help set up a new medical clinic with a non-government organisation.

We had met in Afghanistan in 2001 while I was on tour attached to The British Embassy in Kabul. Jane was working as a paediatric doctor for a medical charity and was living in the same compound. We met during one of many insurgent

11

attacks on the compound, and fate brought us together yet again in the most dramatic and bizarre ways.

I was into the final hour of a long twelve-hour night shift in the control room; I had received credible intelligence at three in the morning about a possible attack on a British compound in Kabul. I had spent the early hours ensuring all coalition forces and agencies were informed and any details to potential targets were to be cancelled. At zero six, forty-five hours, my 'oppo' was in and fully briefed to take over the day shift; a quick handover, and then I went to my room to get some much-needed sleep. As I made my way just across the compound and out of the Embassy gates, I noticed a beautiful young olive-skinned woman walking towards the Gurkha soldiers who were guarding the main entrance off Wazir Akbar Khan Road with a tray of coffees; she had a familiar look about her, 'maybe she's a diplomat I thought.' As I continued to look to figure out why she seemed so friendly, I caught her eye; I turned away, embarrassed that she may have seen me looking at her for a second too long and thinking, 'What a weirdo.' As I passed the Ambassador's house, the two adopted Afghan dogs, Grenade and Jimpy, came running up to me for their usual morning treat, a cookhouse sausage from the previous evening's tea, as I bent down to give them a little stroke before heading off to my bed the boom of a rocket-propelled grenade being launched sounded far too close for comfort. I watched it fly over the compound, missing the British Embassy and landing off the Wazir Akbar Roundabout.

I was knocked off my feet by the impact of a second rocket-propelled grenade that had hit a car within the embassy compound, which then subsequently exploded; I jumped up immediately and had a quick 'check, all my limbs are there, pat down' and as I gathered myself,

I remembered the familiar women who had been heading in the direction of the front gate. I sprang into action, cocking my rifle as I ran towards the front entrance; I could see the young woman kneeling on the floor next to a Gurkha who had been thrown from his position in the observation point and appeared to be injured, as I got to them I could see the Gurkha had a broken foot and the young lady was tending to him, before I could speak she turned and said ' I'm Jane, I'm a doctor can you get a stretcher for this guy he's broke his foot, she was bleeding from a cut on her head from what I assumed was debris from the blast, but she took no time to care for herself and was fixated on helping the Gurkha guard. 'Your bleeding, I said, let me dress that for you 'as I pulled out a field dressing, 'I'm fine, it's just a scratch,' she said, 'this guy is more of a priority.'

Suddenly, a burst of automatic fire rattled the ground just meters away from us; I grabbed Jane and shoved her towards the entrance to a house to take cover. As we got into the safety of the house's walled garden, I shared with some other close protection guys and girls. They came running out and ushered us into the house.

I looked towards Jane and said, 'Are you okay,' her response caught me off guard, 'No, not that guy needed my help, and you just grabbed me away from treating a casualty.'

'I'm sorry, I said, but that guy has a weapon to protect himself, and his buddies will get him to safety. I know you're a doctor, but I couldn't leave you out there unarmed, and a thank you would have been nice,' I said sarcastically. It was perfect timing for one of the Corporals from the ambassador's protection team, who entered the room just when I was about to get a slap from Jane or severely chastised. 'Guys and girls, we have insurgents through the perimeter wall, and we must lockdown here until the compound is safe. Are any of you unarmed? Have you got any weapons training? This is about to get a bit hairy, and we need all hands on deck. I thought, 'Please do not give the attractive doctor a weapon when I've just pissed her off.

I've had weapons training on both sidearms and rifles, so throw me anything, and I'll help you keep the bad guys out said Jane; I was beginning to learn that this innocent and beautiful doctor was a bit of a badass and thought it time to break the ice with a joke ' well I suppose I best not piss you off again Jane, you sound like quite a handy doc, I'm Ginny by the way, and I'm sorry about earlier, Jane smirked and jokingly said 'no problem, just don't ever shove me away from a casualty again or you may find yourself needing a doctor too.' For a moment, our eyes caught each other. I just couldn't put my finger on what was so familiar about this woman as I went to ask her if we'd met before one of the close protection girls burst through the door and said, 'Anyone a medic? We've got a local guard seriously injured,' Jane

17

sprang into action, again without a single thought for herself; I followed as I felt an overwhelming urge to protect her.

This attack lasted eight hours, and it seemed as if I was fully kitted up, as I had just come off duty. I was told to stay and defend the house and any clients in there, but Jane had other intentions. I suppose it's a doctor thing, and I'd be the same knowing I could help anyone injured. Still, the instruction had been given to lock down and protect the house and all persons in it until the attack ended. Still, that would never happen with Jane, so I spent the next eight hours moving from house to house throughout the embassy, protecting Jane as she tended to casualties from the attack. I knew I would get in deep shit for it, but there was no alternative as Jane was going with protection or not. As we came to the

Ambassador's compound, Grenade and Jimpy

appeared. I thought, 'This isn't the time for

sausages, guys. ' Both of them began barking and

seemed to be telling us to follow them; as I

attempted to try to quieten them, unsure of

whether an insurgent was nearby, they ran off

towards the 'Ambo's house' and then stopped at

the open front door and looked back at me, I

turned to Jane. I said, 'Can we check this out?

I've got a feeling the dogs want us to follow,'

'Yes, of course,' she replied; there could be a

casualty. As I entered the ambo's house, I wanted

to shout out naturally, 'Is anyone injured.' Still,

my intuition told me not to. As I turned to walk

into the main corridor of the house, I heard a

burst of automatic fire, and then everything went

black.

As I opened my eyes and looked up, slightly dazed and confused, I immediately tried to sit up, remembering I had gone into the ambo's house with Jane; it was a wrong move, as I was connected to all kinds of IVs and had an intubation tube in my mouth, I gagged as it was swiftly removed and I was gently pressed down to the lying position as Jane said jokingly ' now it's my turn to shove you, I suddenly realised I was in a hospital bed, and the attack was over as Jane was very attractively dressed in her white doctor's coat.

'Ginny, you were shot in your lower abdomen. It was touch and go for a while, but you're out of the woods now. Just take it easy, and it looks like all the hard work you put into at the gym has paid off; as the bullet lodged in your external obliques, it just couldn't get through that solid muscle, 'Jane joked.

As I looked up at Jane, I wondered again why she looked so familiar. Was it the morphine? Was this whole situation a dream? I felt very spaced out as my eyes slowly drifted back into a morphine-controlled state. I looked towards Jane to give a very raspy 'Thank you'; she acknowledged me with a one-finger salute and a big grin as she said, 'You still haven't figured out why I look so familiar, have you? It is me, Jane. We were in care together.' I could not believe it; she was back in my life after all these years, and I knew that at this moment, that warm fuzzy feeling I had felt back when I was eight years old wasn't down to the morphine.

The next four years seemed to go so quickly; Jane and I got engaged, there was talk about having kids, and life was perfect. I had three months left of my final year of service to the Queen. I was based in The Royal Military Academy Sandhurst on The Army Presentation Team, delivering presentations across the United Kingdom to schools, colleges, and universities. Jane was excelling in medicine, having set up her surgery. She had plans to launch a local community medical centre to educate and fund disadvantaged young people through university to become a doctor. This woman of mine had a heart of pure gold, and my admiration for her as a person was nearly on par with my love for her as my partner.

We had rented an apartment just five minutes from Shoreditch High Street. It was ideal for Jane's surgery and a good base for me as I'd secured a great close protection job for a wealthy family in Kensington; it was expensive, but we were both earning good money, so why not splash out a bit and have a nice place?

The morning Jane left replays in my mind every day; as Jane started to stir, I stroked her hairline and said, 'Good morning beautiful, do you have to go?' I had begged her to let Ritchie go as her protection, but the non-government organisation she was going to help set up the Clinic in Kabul had arranged it through the British Embassy, and even though I knew those guys and girls were some of the best, I just would have felt better if Ritchie had gone. 'It's only four weeks Ginny, and the very last time I promise I will never leave you again and we have forever together,' she smiled as she kissed me on the lips, 'now come on, let's get ready as I have got to be at the Airport in two hours. I held her kiss, and just as I was about to push her playfully back onto the bed, her phone rang; as she looked at the screen with a worried expression, I could tell it was Tommy.

Tommy was an addict and had been in rehab twice already; he was only twenty-two and Jane's only sibling. He, too, had been through the care system like Jane but had let his demons absorb him, whereas Jane had done the opposite; she had worked in a store from the age of fifteen years old, saving every penny to get herself into University to become a Doctor of Medicine and specialise in paediatrics.

As she answered the phone, she walked out of the bedroom, and I was pissed off as I knew it would be another call to borrow money from Jane, so he could go and get off his face. Jane was on the phone for an hour, and I could hear her whole conversation. She was correct that Tommy was asking to borrow money. I was fuming because we had planned to head and have our last breakfast together before she got her flight, but now we would have to head straight to the airport as she would be cutting it fine. Tommy always called when we had something special planned, and I couldn't help being short with Jane when she finally got off the call and came back into the bedroom, panicking that she would miss her flight.

The drive to the airport was a nightmare. We hit traffic on the M25, and by the time we got to the airport, Jane had just thirty minutes to get to the check-in desk; I was livid as I hadn't wanted to rush our last moments together or spend them sulking and even though I knew she was only going to be away for four weeks, I just had a horrible churn in my stomach.

'Ginny, I'm sorry we haven't had time to have breakfast, and it's been rushed, but you know I have to be there for Tommy always; he's my brother; you would do the same for Ritchie,' said Jane with a forgiving smile, before I could stop, my frustration got the better of me as I responded ' Ritchie's not a junkie, Jane, he just drains the life out of you and worries you sick as well as taking your money and it pisses me off,' I knew straight away I had hurt her feelings. Still, Jane had the best way of responding always and just leaned across, kissed me on the forehead, and said, 'I'll call you when I get to the compound, and hopefully you will be a bit more chilled out then, I love you, Ginny, it's you and me forever. As she got out of the car and hurried into the departures terminal, I felt like I'd reacted like a spoilt brat as I beeped and blew her a kiss and mouthed sorry; she smiled as she put up her middle finger; it was our other way of telling each other how much we loved them when one of us had just been a twat.

Once I got back home, I threw on my running kit. I went for a run to clear my head and to pass some time, as it would be about another fifteen hours before Jane called from the safety of the compound; she was flying into Dubai, but with only a short transfer into Kabul International Airport, and then to the American Village on the outskirts of Kabul by the armoured escort. I knew I had to occupy my time for the next fifteen hours; otherwise, I would just go insane until I got her call. Not for one minute of those fifteen hours did I ever imagine that the call from Jane would never come!

I'd fallen asleep on the bed, fully clothed, and as I woke startled to what sounded like a knock on the front door, I glanced at my watch; it was zero three, thirteen. Why hadn't my alarm woken me up as I'd set it so I was awake for Jane's call, which I was expecting around midnight? Maybe she had been delayed. I checked my phone, no message, no calls. I dialled Jane's number, but it rang out! Again, there was a knock at the front door, this time a bit more forceful; whom the fuck was knocking at my door at three in the morning, 'Tommy, I bet it's you,

you prick,' I said out loud to myself as I made my way downstairs to open the door.

As I opened the door, two guys in suits flashed a badge, and my immediate thought was, it's Tommy; he had been arrested, but these guys didn't look like your average coppers, and my heart sank as I realised this had to be related to Jane! 'Ms. Smith, we are so sorry to disturb you at this late hour, but can we come in as we need to speak to you about Ms. Jane Rodgers.' 'Is she okay? What has happened?' I pressed as they walked into the hall. This time, the other guy spoke, 'I'm afraid the embassy detail that was tasked to collect Jane from Kabul Airport got hit on route back to the American Village, and while it has yet to be confirmed, we believe all persons travelling in the vehicle, including Ms Rodgers, have been killed in the attack! My knees buckled, and I fell to the floor; next came the

uncontrollable sobs as I tried to take in being told

that my soulmate, my true love, was dead.

Chapter 2 – Filling the Void.

It had been two years since Jane was cruelly taken from this world; she had everything to give, and this world would have been a better place with her in it. Nothing or no one would ever replace her; she had been my everything, and the guilt I carried from that day of being in a mood and rushing to the airport shattered my heart into a thousand pieces, and I could not find my way out of the darkness.

It's funny how life turns out sometimes; in that last hour, I was annoyed with Jane because her brother Tommy called her asking again to borrow money, which had pissed me off. Yet, I drank with him until I felt nothing while he threw coke up his nose. Since Jane died, I felt like he was my only connection to her, and I knew she would have wanted me to be there for him, but not like this; it wasn't that I was encouraging him, but I wasn't stopping him either.

Tommy lived in Manchester, and I regularly met up with him and got drunk while he got high. Then, as he headed into town, I would head to Canal Street to meet a stranger and have a one-night stand to try to feel 'something.' It never did me any good, but I was lost, and it helped pass the days, nights, months, and years.

I had moved back to the Wirral, and little did I know that Jane had bought the apartment in Shoreditch and was planning on giving me the keys on our anniversary to be our forever home; I know it doesn't seem very empathetic, but I had to sell it and move on as I couldn't face all the memories we had together in it. Jane also had life insurance and had left it to me as there was only Tommy, and she had never found her birth parents; she had also left an ISA account for Tommy, and he had at least done one sensible thing and bought a flat in Manchester with it, but the remaining money that was left, it was safe to say went up his nose.

I had bought a house with the money on the rural side of the Wirral in Thornton Hough; I just wanted to be hidden away from society and have grounds to wander freely. I'd converted an old barn into kennels and took in any stray dogs to avoid being put down because they had overstayed their time in the council kennels. I'd get the dog, which would become another member of the 'hound family.' I'd taken on a young lad, Steven, who was Ritchie's friend's son and had gotten into a bit of trouble with gangs to help with the kennels. He was only eighteen years old and a vulnerable kid whom the local wannabe gangsters could easily manipulate; he was a real grafter and ran the kennels for me. I also gave him the summerhouse to stay in, which he loved. I had turned into his little mancave, and it kept him off the streets and away from trouble.

Ritchie had left the Marines after 12 years' service on a half pension which he used to set up his security firm, and on the days I stayed sober, he threw the odd security job my way, but I'd only take the shitty jobs, sitting in a cabin for 12-14hrs to pick up the extra money and keep things ticking over, as financially I was sorted for another twelve months from what Jane had left me. I couldn't even look after myself, never mind being someone's bodyguard, so the extra money paid for Steven and saved from the savings. Ritchie was my rock; he always picked me up from a random woman's house or off my kitchen floor. A natural joker, he always tried to cheer me up and often joked 'that if I weren't a raving Leza and his adopted sister, then I would have been sorted being his wife'. He only got serious whenever he had to come and pick me up from Tommy's, as he made it quite clear there was no love for Tommy. He hated that I still had him in my life and couldn't understand why I went to stay with him, but he couldn't ever understand as I was holding on to my only connection to Jane. I knew Tommy was no good for me; he played the victim, was brought up in care, turned to drugs, and became an addict, but he was all I had to remember. Jane and I weren't ready to let that go.

I just about managed to exist through another week; I'd done two shifts for Ritchie to stop me heading towards Manchester and a weekend of drinking until I passed out with Tommy; he said he had planned a 'mates date' in Liverpool for us both for the weekend, staying in an apartment on the docks, I agreed to go as to me it was just another forty-eight hours of getting through life without Jane.

I met with Ritchie at Seacombe, and we got the ferry over to Liverpool, checked in the apartment, and then headed out to start the afternoon with some cocktails in the Revolution bar.

It was a lovely summer's day, and I nearly broke into a smile for a split second, sitting in the sun with a Pina Colada and watching Ritchie fail at chatting up a hen party. The Bride of the party turned around as Ritchie was trying the 'my friends a lesbian' chat line, and she had an air of resemblance to Jane. Straight away, my stomach sank, you know, that natural gut-wrenching feeling, to the point I thought I might be sick; I need a shot; I felt so as Ritchie continued to embarrass himself, I took myself to the bar. I downed four shots of tequila. I just wanted this pain to subside and the numbness takes over.

Ritchie patted my back with such force that I spilt my fifth tequila over the bar; I snapped, 'Ritchie, you fookin, bellend, what was the need for that? Ritchie tried to make a joke of it. 'Oh come on ya soft melt, cheer the fuck up, look at all these women wanting a bit of the Ritchster, and you are in with a chance as two of them are lezza's'. 'Cheer the fuck up, Ritchie, are you fooking messing? Did you not notice that the girl you are chatting with looks like Jane? Stop joking around for once and have a fookin heart,'

Ritchie looked hurt, but before he could respond, I nudged past him and said I'm going outside for some fresh air.

As I stood looking out across the Mersey, I just wanted a wave to swallow me up, wash me away and take me to Jane. It was tempting, but in all honesty, I didn't have the bottle to end my life; even though I thought about it so many times, I could never follow it through as Jane would never forgive me as she dedicated her life to saving people's lives and for me to take my own would be the biggest insult to her. It worried me that she wouldn't be there to meet me if I took my own life. So, a couple of minutes of fresh air. Then, as I was about to head back into the bar for another five shots to numb the pain, my phone rang; it was Tommy.

I answered, 'Ginny, it's Tommy; guess where I am?' I replied, 'In some crack den, with a bag of Charlie? 'Hahaha, you got the Charlie bit right; I'm in Liverpool, you raving lesbian. Where are you? Let's meet up?'

Within minutes Tommy had joined me outside 'Revs' shortly after Ritchie walked out, and I could instantly see he was pissed off to see Tommy. 'What the fuck is he doing here, Ginny,' for fucks sake, can't you just leave her alone, Tommy. 'Fuck you, meathead', Tommy replied; I just knew what was about to come next as I could tell already that Tommy was high, and as he launched towards Ritchie, Ritchie responded first and caught Tommy square in the jaw with a right hook which sent him crashing into a nearby table and sent everyone's drinks flying.

I knew it was wrong to go to Tommy's defence instantly, but I couldn't help but scream at Ritchie, 'What are you playing at? What was the need for that? Just fuck off, Ritchie, you out of order; again, that hurt look appeared on Ritchie's face; I had to get Tommy away, so I just left. As we walked across town, Tommy was laughing as the drugs started to numb the impact from Ritchie's punch, 'he calls himself a Marine, he punches like a girl, no offence meant Ginny, 'Oh shut up, Tommy, come on let's go in here and can you just behave please as I need a drink'. We headed into the Beaconsfield, and I continued to drown the night away; I downed shot after shot and took my drinking to a new level. I forgot about Ritchie; the alcohol absorbed me, and I didn't hesitate to think how he had tried to do something nice for me for the weekend, and yet here I was again with Tommy, getting so drunk that I would eventually pass out and god knows where I would wake up.

I woke up in Tommy's flat not having any idea how I had got there, but, yet, I suppose it was better than a random's house as I'm sure Ritchie would be in no mood to come and get me this time as I had deserted him last night for Tommy. I got up and realised I was still half pissed, it was eleven thirty, and as I headed to the kitchen to get some water, I noticed a picture of Tommy and Jane; my heart sank, the gut-wrenching

feeling took over, so instead of the tap, I went for a half-drunk bottle of vodka and took a swig; whilst Tommy slept, I finished the bottle off and then drifted off into another alcohol-induced coma.

I can't tell you much about what happened for those three months I spent at Tommy's; as I just woke each morning and threw another bottle of vodka down my neck, I'd hit an all-time low, and to be honest, the only good that came from it was Tommy got that concerned he stopped the drugs and cared for me, it eventually led to him calling Ritchie as he didn't know how to deal with me. Ritchie was still angry and hadn't answered, so Tommy had left a message. What I can tell you is that I was self-destructing; I didn't want to carry on. What did I have to live for? Every day was just another day of hitting the bottle, and then one night, in another alcohol-induced coma, I dreamt about Jane.

She came to me so clearly, as beautiful as ever, but the look on her face told me she was not happy with me. I reached out, and she held my hand; I could feel her warmth, and she pulled me in close and whispered into my ear, 'Don't give up Ginny, my love'; you have so much more to give this world, we will be together again one day, but not now, please be strong, keep going and stop being a twat to Ritchie, he's your rock, and he will get you through this.

Her hold started to ease, and as I went to pull her back in, not wanting ever to let her go, I grabbed at fresh air; just like that, she was gone again, and I was back in Tommy's flat on the floor with an empty bottle next to me, I wish I could be substantial, the dream had seemed so natural, but the only reality that hit me was that I was drunk, I had gone into the lowest depths of my life, and I had no idea how to crawl out of the

massive dark hole I was trapped in.

Chapter 3 – Back in the game

In the three months I had spent with Tommy, I had lost weight through constant drinking and hardly eating; Jane had come to me frequently in my dreams, and last night, she joked about how my abs would have no chance of stopping a bullet now, I'd let both my physical appearance and mental state deteriorate, and although I looked so much forward each night to dreaming of Jane, I knew she was trying to get through to me. What hit me the hardest and made me realise I needed to change my current lifestyle was that I was letting Jane down.

At that moment, I thought, right, I need to go and try to lead some life; the pain of losing Jane was still so raw, but the thought of letting her down again was too much; I'd already done that once and lost her, so now was the time to start fighting back and try to get something that just resembled a little bit of the old me back.

Tommy had been clean for over two months due to his worries about me and my mental decline. He had tried every trick in the book, and today, he came into the living room where my makeshift bed was. He said, 'Ginny, I've been thinking; I'd like to get into my Phys, so how's about we both start running and doing a few workouts? I couldn't believe my ears. Tommy had never so much broken into a quick march, never mind go for a run; although naturally slim (probably due to the number of drugs he took), he was such an unfit and bone idol. At that moment, I thought that maybe Jane was coming to him too, in his sleep. He was shocked when I said, OK then, mate, let's go, no time like the present, before he could make an excuse, as I don't think he was expecting that response, we were off down for a run to Salford Quays, it was painful for us both and as we got back to his flat and collapsed on the floor, red-faced and out of breath, we laughed and made each other a promise there and then that this was a time for us to both get back on track.

I returned home and realised how much I had just left people in the shit; Steven had done a sterling job in managing the kennels, no doubt under instruction from Ritchie, but equally, he was a cracking lad and maturing into a fine young man. Tommy had decided to leave Manchester to leave behind the temptation and evil influences. He had asked if he could come and stay to keep our fitness regime going and that he wanted to sell his flat and buy a gym as he had just enrolled on a two-week personal trainer course, it was only going to be a temporary thing whilst he found his place and with a four-bedroom house that only occupied little old me, I was glad he had asked as this new Tommy showed me how much he was like Jane. It hit me why she had stuck up for him all those years, as she knew Tommy without drugs, and he was a real sweetheart.

I knew it would not take long for Ritchie to hear I was back through Steven's dad, and I knew I had to make up for how I had behaved towards him; I loved Ritchie deeply, like a brother, and I knew how much I would have hurt him, so for him to hear I'd brought Tommy back with me I knew he would assume he was still taking drugs and he would stay away. I couldn't take the shithouse way out and text him out of the blue after three months of nothing, so I sucked it up and gave him a call; as the call rang out, I could almost picture him staring at his phone, wanting to pick up so desperately but so hurt that he didn't know what to say, as it went to his cheery voicemail I left probably the most extended and most heartfelt message ever, it went something like this:

' Hi Ritchie, listen I'm not expecting you to forgive me overnight, I've been the biggest fuck up ever, and I don't want to play the world's smallest violin to gain sympathy when I've been the biggest twat ever, I just want you to know I'm back home and I've got a clean and fitness freak Tommy with me, it's only temporary as he's buying a gym and getting his own place, here on the Wirral, he's really making a go of it and he has been my carer for the past three months and has really changed his life around, anyway I know you won't grow to love him but you may actually just start to like him a little bit when you see the new Tommy, anyway enough about Tommy, I'm calling you because I've had such a big void in my life through losing Jane and what I've realised is I can't lose you, your my bestest friend in the whole world, my brother in arms and you've always been the brother I never had and I want you to know I am so sorry for hurting you and I just want you to know I Love you and I hope you can forgive me and when you're ready I'd love to meet up for a brew and put everything right'

The following two weeks passed, and I had still not heard from Ritchie, but Steven had mentioned he was out in Dubai on the job, so I hoped that it was just because he hadn't read it yet and would get in touch once he got home. Every day, Tommy would head out for a run across the sandhills in Moreton; I had to give it to Tommy. He was getting fit, and he was focused on starting fresh; he was in the final stages of buying a decent gym, and although I'd assumed he had thrown most of his inheritance from Jane up his nose, he hadn't, and he had always kept a little nest egg that he was now using to set up a gym. I was starting to feel so much fitter myself, and helping Tommy get his gym set up was keeping me on track and giving me something to focus on; I'd picked up some door work in Birkenhead to keep the money coming in more than anything and also to keep my skills as fresh as I could, I was doing Thursday, Fridays and

51

Saturdays and trust me Birkenhead was the place to keep up to pace with your conflict management skills as every night there was at least twelve fights per hour. I worked the door with a Syrian lad called Liam; he was a top lad and properly tried to look after me and keep me away from the rough asses but on his first encounter of me 'dealing' with a 'sted head' kicking off let's say he was impressed and literally from that moment on would say 'go on Ginny, you can deal with that one, as he knew I could more than handle myself'.

It was a Friday night, and I was running slightly late as one of the dogs had needed to go the vet as they had been vomiting, so I'd let Liam know I was going to be slightly late; he'd told me not to worry as the club was empty. I got to the club eventually, and it was surprised as it was booming, 'fookin hell Liam, why didn't you say I'd of got Steven to sort the dog? You must be run off your feet; Liam was a massive animal lover, and as much as he looked the part of a doorman, he was a big softie when it came to animals, so straight away he replied, 'No way Ginny, your puppy comes first', anyway it's a private function. They have been no problem at all; some guy has booked the whole club for the night, no locals, invite-only, and to be fair, he's a proper sound guy, he's got his own security firm, and he's dropped me a card and said if I want to get into close protection give him a shout, plus he's got me Pepsi on tap, so think it's an easy night for us tonight.

As I went to walk into the club to see who this 'big licks' was, someone nudged into me, it was only Ritchie, ' fancy seeing you here ya big lezza, well don't just stand there, give a brother a hug, if you meant everything you said on that voicemail you soppy melt', I didn't even have to think about an apology I could see he had already forgiven me, but I let my guard down for once and gave him a big hug and whispered into his ear, 'this is the only time you will ever get me saying this, but I love you Ritchie, and I'm so sorry', now what the fuck are you celebrating, hiring this gaff out?

Ritchie went on to explain how he had just won a high-value contract out in Dubai, and it would be a big job that would put his company on the map for international agreements. If this was a success, he wanted me to join the celebration. Still, I told him I couldn't as I was working and he better behave, to which he responded, 'Well, I might be a tit, just for a bit of payback for your behaviour, then laughed and said, listen 'I've had a few too many already and don't want to go into detail on the job whilst I'm pissed, so let's catch up for that coffee tomorrow as no way am I letting you continue to work on a door in Birkenhead, you know your too good for that Ginny, but it's good to see you back on track, so bell me tomorrow as I'll probably need a wakeup call but let's meet about one o clock yeah?'.

At about twelve forty-five, I got to Costa on the Croft Retail Park and was surprised to see Ritchie perched on a stool by the window. 'You keen after a night on it.' Your dodgy dad dancing was on point last night, I joked, 'All I can remember, ginny, are you telling me how much you loved me and begging me to be ya bezzy again,' said Ritchie. 'Anyway, sit down. I've already got you a de-caff flat white; is that a lezza thing? I want you in on this job, Ginny; it is made for you,' the excitement in Ritchie's voice was intriguing, so for once, I followed his instruction and took a seat and a sip of my coffee.

'I've got an easy gig for you, Ginny,' Ritchie said, 'good pay, few months in Dubai, all expenses paid, looking after a rich bitch whilst she visits her Father, she isn't too bad on the eye and wait for the best bit rumour is 'she's a raving lezza like you, so you might even get ya fingers wet if you're lucky', here you go, I've done a draft op order, cast your eyes on that' Ritchie had such a way with words.

As I read the op order, I reviewed the information on the 'client.'

Ellen Fatima Shervani, age forty years old, an Irish/Iranian businesswoman, has several properties: one in Kensington, London, an inherited family estate in Killiney, County Dublin and an estate in Jumeirah, Dubai, where she is currently residing for a six-month visit to see her father, Amir Shervani.

A six-month all-expenses trip to Dubai whilst earning a shit load of cash would appeal to anyone in the game, and literally, gigs like this are scarce. However, I hated Dubai; being in a country that treats homosexuality as a punishable crime is never a good move for a lesbian whose most recent favourite pastime is getting shitfaced and sleeping with random women. So, as lucrative as the job was, I wasn't that interested until I flicked over the page, and there she was in a striking picture: Elle Shervani, one of the most beautiful women I had ever set eyes on; she had the perfect genes of the Irish and Iranians, olive-skinned with dark hair and the most piercing blue eyes I have ever seen. Ritchie laughed and said there it is, hook, line and sinker,' the temptation to get ya tongue in between those fine legs is too much to say no. 'Shut up, you tit Ritchie, can't you just take it down a little bit? You know the biggest rule to never break in CP is to sleep with a client; now get me another coffee and a cheese and ham toastie, and I might think about it.

As I read the rest of the op order, Ritchie watched me from the queue with that smug look; he knew I wouldn't say no. I thought I got to the final page, which was blank but had Team India

Bravo at the top, but then Ritchie did love his phonetic alphabet. As I placed it back on the table without a second thought, Ritchie grabbed it and said, 'Here ya go, lezza, get that down ya neck,' and attempted to distract me with a cheese and ham toastie. Still, now of his reaction, I was intrigued.

'What's Team India Bravo Ritchie,' 'Oh nothing, just messing around with Team names', Ritchie replied, 'so it's not just the girl,' we are looking after?' I questioned. Suddenly for probably only the second time since meeting Ritchie back in care, he got all serious on me; he paused for a moment and then said, 'Shit, I picked that up by mistake, listen, Ginny, you know I trust you more than anyone in the world, but the guys I'm working for have clearly stated I'll lose the contract if the real reason we are going to Dubai gets out, I just can't tell you yet, at the moment it's a 'need to know' basis, and all you need to know is that your BG for Ms Shervani. When the time's right, I will tell you everything, I promise. 'Ok, keep ya undies on, big lad, no problem, I will just get you pissed before we go, and you will blurt it all out anyway, I joked. 'Fuck off Ginny,' now eat that toastie before I do, Ritchie snapped. By Ritchie's response, I got the impression there was a bit more to this job, but I wasn't too interested as I knew he would tell me eventually, so Dubai for six months was.

We needed to be in Dubai in three weeks, which didn't leave much time, but then Steven had done a great job with the kennels with no notice when I'd lost my head, so I knew I had no problem there, and the more I thought about it, I started to feel a bit excited to be 'back in the game'. Ritchie had some odd security jobs he needed picking up here and there over the next couple of weeks, so I helped him out as it beat standing on a door of a nightclub in Birkenhead any day; Steven was fine with keeping house again, to be honest I think he loved having the place to himself, he was a quiet lad but had recently met a nice girl and was in the romancing stage so having a big house in the middle of nowhere to himself was ideal for him.

I remembered the night I'd seen Ritchie again when he was throwing a big party to celebrate winning the Dubai Job. It only hit me that there were quite a few 'spooks' looking guys at the party. It started to intrigue me more about who and what Team India Bravo was, so I rang

Ritchie and arranged to meet him over in Liverpool on Friday night before we flew down to Gatwick from Manchester on the following Monday and then onto Dubai, I suddenly wondered why we were not going direct from Manchester. Still, I think everything seemed intriguing now I knew there was more to the job. I'd get all the info from Ritchie after a few cocktails on Friday night.

Chapter 4 – The Dubai Job

'I'm sorry Ginny', there's been a slight change to the plan we will have to go to London on Friday and stay there the weekend until the flight on Monday as there is a briefing on Sunday and the guys want us there' said Ritchie, this made things even more strange a briefing before 'wheel's down' the usual script is a briefing once in place to go through BG detail which most of it had been covered in the Op Order as it was just a simple BG job looking after Ms Sharvani, I was speculative, but just agreed as Ritchie sounded a bit vexed. 'I've booked us into a nice pad in Kensington, don't worry, I know you can't resist me, but it's a two bed so you will have your own room, Ritchie joked, although I could tell by his voice that was an effort not to give away that he was a little stressed. 'Flights from Manchester are at eighteen fifteen hours on Friday, so I'll pick you up on route if ya want in a taxi about fifteen hundred?' 'Yes, that's a sound, big lad, and I guess we best keep it professional then and stay off the ale,' I joked. Again, there was a nervous tone to Ritchie's normal jovial response. 'Yeah, defo Ginny, we can't fuck this one up, seriously this is going to put my firm on the international map seriously, so can you be on your best behaviour, please' asked Ritchie, 'hahaha I'm always professional on a job lad, you know that I won't let you down' I reassured Ritchie.

From the moment I got in the cab with Ritchie, I could feel the nervousness, so I played the part as it was clear this job meant a lot to his business, and even winding him up seemed a bit cruel whilst he was clearly under pressure to deliver, so I just struck up a general conversation. 'So, Ritchie, just me and you? I am not fishing for whatever else you are up to; I am just making a general convo and wondering if anyone I know will join us. 'There are a couple of guys you don't know also ex-boot necks; they will meet us at the briefing on Sunday, but no other females for you, I'm afraid, so it's a dry op all around for you' again another attempt at hiding his nervousness. Still, I was feeling a bit sly on him as I'd never seen him like this before, so I just played along, 'Well, you said the clients a lezza, so I might have a slight chance at not being dry for the whole six months' I laughed, ' You crack on lezza, but I'm not bailing you out of a Dubai prison, I'm not that minted' replied Ritchie as he eased a little with resuming our usual banter.

Throughout the short flight to Gatwick, Ritchie was on his laptop; I assumed he was doing the 'paperwork'. He had one of those screen covers on his laptop, so I couldn't even see what he was doing, and I held back from challenging him and just got the op order out and went over it again; there was just something about Elle Sharvani that captivated me and I don't just mean her striking looks, there was something about her sea blue eyes that had a hint of sadness to them. I couldn't help but wonder about what it was.

At that moment, I realised that for the past week, whilst I had been preparing for Dubai, I had hardly stopped to think about Jane, and a sudden wave of guilt took over me.

Ritchie slammed his laptop shut, 'wheels down fifteen minutes lezza', he seemed a bit chirpier; maybe it was the paperwork as I know he hated that side of the job; as an ex-marine, his op orders were shit hot, but he had always stressed over them as he wanted them to be perfect and he always preferred to be in the thick of the action, not pen–pushing as he would say. 'Sound, how we getting to the pad?' I asked. 'a car is picking us up. Suppose you need anything or want to go and grab some food. In that case, we've got a driver until Monday,' but please, Ginny, if you venture into Soho, please keep a lid on it and don't take the piss; my client has provided the driver, so don't go on a mad one please, begged Ritchie, 'ok man, I get the drift, I won't show you up, the chill will ya' I laughed. 'Where are we staying again? Just so I can have a little gander at what plenty of fish has to offer, it seems as if I am

67

going to be dry for six months,' I asked, ' Mexham Gardens in Kensington, the pad is, your POF date will be impressed, but do me a favour and only have someone round Saturday as I'll be with the client until early hours' said Ritchie, ' Jeez, I was joking. However, now I know I'm not invited to wherever you're going on Saturday night, I might do that,' I said; again, I was intrigued that there was more to this job as usually Ritchie couldn't hold his piss. Still, he genuinely seemed stressed to be keeping whatever it was from me; I thought to myself, fuck it, I'm looking for a 'hook up' for Saturday as I will drive myself insane staying in, wondering what Ritchie is up to.

The driver who picked us up was your typical 'grey man' as known in the close protection world; he had ex-copper written all over him, in his mid-fifty, so probably not long retired after a twenty-year stint and spoke with a gentle Mancunian accent. He was driving a Range Rover, and as I gestured, 'Nice motor mate', he replied, 'Oh, this is firm, I drive a Bentley' 'Smug twat, I thought, but replied, 'Oh, they must pay you well then, maybe I need to move to London, whereabouts in Manchester are you from?', I could see him glancing over to Ritchie and then quickly to me in the rear-view, he paused briefly then replied 'Droylsden originally but been in London the past four years', ' I'm not being speculative, but ex greater Manchester police at a guess?', I questioned, 'god, you ask a lot of questions don't you, something like that yes, my name's Gregg before you ask' he laughed. I was only conversing as it was just over an hour's drive; Gregg was an amiable chap. Still, it didn't give much away and diverted a lot of the conversation when it was about himself, but chatting away made the journey to Kensington a bit quicker. I was checking whether I could trust this guy after a few sherbets as he would likely be bringing me and a 'plus one' back on Saturday night, but he didn't seem like a snitch, so I'd be okay.

We got to Mexham Gardens just after eight p.m. It looked like a wealthy part of Kensington, and the pad was one of those mansions-looking houses just off a high street. 'Jeez, Ritchie, you weren't messing when you said I'd be impressed; this gaff must have cost you an arm and a leg', I said. Before Ritchie could respond, Gregg replied, 'Well, the boss does treat us all well', doesn't he, Ritch?' Ritchie shot Gregg a concerned look like he shouldn't have said it. I immediately thought to myself, what the fuck has Ritchie got us into? I hope this isn't some dodgy underground gig.' Ritchie knew precisely what I was thinking by the look on my face and said, 'Trust me, Ginny, you will know everything as soon as I can elaborate, and I'll let you in on everything.' he then gestured to Gregg. ' I was just about to tip you then big mouth; maybe I should speak to the boss about your discretion', Gregg looked slightly concerned. Still, he didn't respond, and Ritchie threw him a fifty-pound note anyway. I couldn't help but wonder about what this job was all about as there was more to it, and I had never seen Ritchie so focused on a job but yet at the same time so 'on edge.'

The apartment was fantastic, exactly what you would expect from this area of Kensington; my room was on the second floor and pretty much occupied the whole floor, it had a massive on-suite with one of those old-fashioned stand-alone baths, and as I opened the patio door I ventured out onto a fully decked private veranda with a hot tub and an incredible view across London as I walked back in Ritchie was standing there looking all smug, 'impressed aren't ya lezza, imagine the shag you're gonna get off whoever you bring back here tomorrow night, she's gonna be pussy, I mean putty in your hands' he laughed' then he got all serious 'this job is it

Ginny', this is the making of us I promise, so just get a shag out your system tomorrow, and then please be on your best behaviour for this job as I need your full attention on this one. 'Ok, if you insist on me hooking up, I will.' I was going to order a meal and have a quiet night in' but since you are persuading me to do otherwise, throw that Gregg another fifty note to take me to Soho tomorrow,' I said playfully. Ritchie lunged at me, and rugby tackled me to the bed as he always tried to when we were teenagers and ended up as he always did when we were play fighting as teenagers with my legs around his neck, begging me not to choke him out. I loved this guy like no other, and I knew that whatever this job was, he would never put me in danger or get me involved in something dodgy, so I just put it to the back of my head and thought I'd find out soon enough as

I trusted Ritchie with my life. We headed out for some food and then got an early night, ready to venture into Soho and see what my final one-night stand would be before six months of celibacy.

I woke up about seven in the morning, as I'd planned my day: a quick run, then have a workout in the gym that was in the basement, and then a nice bath before heading into Soho at about three clocks, the briefing wasn't until twenty hundred hours on Sunday, and I wasn't planning on drinking too much as I wanted a fresh head. I expected Ritchie to be up already and eating breakfast, so I headed down to the kitchen to see if he was up for joining me for a run. Walking into the kitchen, I noticed a note on the table that read.

'Morning, Lezza. Sorry, I am up and out early today, finalising a few things with the

client, so don't expect me back until the early hours. I enjoy having the place to

yourself and your booty call, but do me a favour and don't be hungover for the

briefing tomorrow, or I'll slap you; love the most handsome bloke you know, Ritchie

xxx.'

I suddenly realised that for these past few weeks of preparing for this job again, I'd hardly thought about Jane, even to the point that I hadn't realised the place we were staying in was just six miles away from our old apartment on Shoreditch High Street and the run I was about to go on would take me past our old house. I should have felt that same feeling of guilt I had a few weeks ago, but I didn't this time; I felt the opposite, like I'd finally started to find some peace and that although I missed her terribly, she was also sending me a message that it was time to find myself and live my life and move on.

I grabbed my earphones and phone and searched for a playlist, and as I headed out on my run, the first song that came on was 'You to Me Are Everything' by The Real Thing. I couldn't believe it; this was mine and Jane's song, and at that very moment, it confirmed she was with me and wanted me to get on with my life. I felt sad yet happy and motivated at the same time. She would always be my guardian angel and had only left my side physically. I whispered, 'I love you forever, Jane; please keep guiding me.'

I ran just short of eight miles, and it was the best I had felt in a very long time; I followed up with a core circuit for forty minutes in the gym and then by the time I had got a bath, I got ready and had something to eat it was almost half three, and I hadn't even had a chance to find a 'hook up', so I went onto POF and done a few swipes before I found an attractive blonde called Becky who funnily enough was only a few miles away. So, I sent her a message asking if she wanted to meet later. Should I have been alerted by the instant response with a 'yes? She Bar at five o clock? But I wasn't assed, I only wanted a bit of company, so I responded 'Great, see you then', I'd taken Gregg's number and gave him a quick call to make sure he was free to drop me off and then pick me up later, which he was as he had been instructed to make sure he was at my 'beck and call', and he would pick me up at half four as it was only a twenty-minute drive into Soho, so I finished off getting ready. If I got lucky, I had a quick, tidy round and ensured the hot tub was on for a little dip later.

As I walked into the bar, I cast my eyes around quickly to make sure I was there before Becky as it was a common thing to be looking for someone who looked nothing like their profile picture, so I always asked them to let me know how to identify them by a pink scarf or something else that would point them out, so I could pitch up by the window and then get off if Becky was Barry. Becky had said she would be wearing a bright red duffle-type coat and matching red bobble hat, and I instantly thought, well, at least she's wearing the right colour. I noticed her enter the bar, and I couldn't believe she looked just as attractive as she did in her profile picture; this was an excellent start to the evening'. I waved across to her, and from the look on her face, I read that she also appeared pleasantly surprised that I looked the same as my profile picture. I never put my real name on my profile in my industry. Hence, as she greeted me with an attractive smile and said, 'Hi Jenny, I'm Becky', I almost forgot about my cover name, but quickly regained myself with 'Hi Becky, I hope you don't mind, but I've already got us a bottle of prosecco as I noticed it was one of your favourite drinks', cheesy I know. Still, it diverted her attention and gave me time to remember my name for tonight was Jenny.

The conversation flowed quite freely, and Becky seemed like an adorable girl. For a moment, I felt guilty that my initial intention had been to get her in the hot tub and have some company for the night as per my usual hookups, but as we chatted away, I felt like I'd known her for ages. I was conscious not to get too drunk. We just talked away for a couple of hours with no mention of previous relationships or bad 'hookups', just a good conversation about what we both did for a living (obviously, mine was a cover story of just being a Security guard for a corporate business) and what our interests were. When I checked my watch, it was twenty-one thirty; I couldn't believe we had been chatting for over four hours and only got through one bottle of prosecco. Becky caught me checking my watch and jokingly said, 'Sorry, am I keeping you from another date?' 'No, not at all; honestly, I can't believe we have been chatting for over four hours and only just finished one bottle of prosecco. Most of my hookups, I've either done a runner, they've done a runner or were four bottles in by now,' I joked, 'Well, I'll take that as a compliment that I'm good company,' laughed Becky. 'Do you want another drink?' I asked what was wrong with me; at this stage, I would usually say, "Do you want to come back to mine for a drink, but it was different tonight for some reason. Was it the job was keeping me on my toes, or did I have a soft spot for this girl? Becky's response threw me as she said, 'It depends whether you are asking, do I want a drink here, or are you suggesting we go to yours or mine for a more private drink?' She caught me off guard. I think I even blushed. Come on,

Ginny, pull your head together. You came out for a one-night stand, and you're getting offered one; what's wrong with you? I chastised myself silently in my head before responding; before I could react, Becky laughed and said, 'Oh, sorry, did you just blush?' again trying to regain myself, I replied, 'I think I did; I'm easy either way, what do you prefer?', as Becky nearly spat out her last mouthful of Prosecco due to my response I thought what the fuck have I just said and someone pass me a spade. Becky again top trumped me with her response and said, 'Well, if you're easy, I suggest we go back to your place', right Come on, regain yourself, Ginny; I counted to three in my head and responded coolly, ' ok, my place it is then, just let me call us a ride', I called Gregg and asked him to come and pick me up, he joked and a plus one by any chance, hope

she's hot, ' Fuck off and hurry up ya perv' I
replied.

The story I 'd told Becky was that the
corporate company I worked for had picked me
and another colleague as 'employee of the year'
and had put us up in an exclusive apartment in
Kensington for the weekend and that we also had
a private driver for the night as we were heading
home tomorrow night. Quite rightly, she had
asked about my colleague, and as I knew Ritchie
would be out, I said he had met up with mates
and was out. I know it sounded a bit ropey, but
she fell for it and didn't seem suspicious at all.
Then I had to remember she wasn't me, who was
wary of anyone I met for the first time, but then it
suddenly dawned on me that I had no suspicions
about Becky either. As Gregg pulled up in the

Range Rover and jumped out to open the door with a polite 'Evening ladies, I'm your driver to get you both home safely', Becky glanced across and said jokingly ', I think I might just have to meet up with you again if this is the service you get for employee of the year,' Gregg looked across at me and winked as Becky got into the car.

For the sixteen-minute drive from Soho to Mexham Gardens, Becky chatted to Gregg, who was lapping up the conversation as he talked about how he was a Police Officer from Droylsden. I started to think, Hang on a minute. You weren't this chatty when I got in the car yesterday and was throwing questions your way, yet here you are, practically telling Becky your life story. Still, then it struck me how infectious her personality was. Although I had only had the equivalent of half a bottle of prosecco, I started to question whether I had given anything away as she certainly had a way of making you feel like you had known her all your life.

As we pulled outside the apartment, I asked Becky if she wanted to come in for a drink. I won't be offended if you don't want to, and I can get you a lift home from our friendly driver?' 'Jenny, I've been driven in a Range Rover to a plush part of Kensington. I want to see the inside of this place, so your answer is no, I'm not going home just yet', Becky laughed. 'Ok, let's go then,' Thanks, Mr. Driver, you've been a darling, I said sarcastically, 'Wait a minute, these are from the boss', said Gregg as he handed over two bottles of Dom Perignon. 'Oh, this just gets better', smirked Becky; I looked at Gregg as if to say, 'What the fuck,' but he just gestured ', have fun, don't do anything I wouldn't do and pulled off.

As we walked into the apartment and Becky gave a running commentary on how gorgeous it was, I thought to myself, Right, get a grip now, Ginny, you've got an attractive girl, two bottles of Dom, a Hot tub and the boss, whoever that may be has just encouraged you to get drunk further by gifting the bottles of Dom. Lost in those thoughts for a moment, I'd not noticed that Becky had suddenly disappeared; as I went to grab a corkscrew, she suddenly appeared with two glasses, bottle of Dom already open, so

I thought fuck it, let loose Ginny, this girl is definitely up for it.

'I noticed the private veranda and hot tub, Jenny; I hope you have something more practical for me to slip into,' Becky joked; the right time to get your game on Ginny, I thought as I replied, 'Actually, I don't, so I'm afraid for both of us it's going to have to be just our underwear if you want to try the hot tub out', 'oh, someone is starting to get brave' joked Becky, well I'm up for that she said as she stripped down to her underwear and made her way into the hot tub before she could take the piss out of me further, and equally to show willing, I followed her lead and stripped down to my underwear and grabbed the bottle of Dom and headed into the hot tub.

I woke up in still my underwear, and as I rolled across the other side of the bed, I suddenly realised the only reason the sheets were damp was that I'd slept in my wet underwear after getting into the hot tub; I could just about recall getting into bed, but strangely I didn't have that much of a bad head. However, I had no recollection of Becky leaving until I noticed a scribbled post-it on the bedside table which read.

'Thanks for a good night, lightweight. Don't worry; Your driver gave me a lift home since you crashed out on me; who knows, you may be lucky enough to meet me again, Becky X.'

I thought to myself, 'How the fuck did she know to call Gregg, but before my thoughts wandered further, Ritchie came barging into the room. 'Ginny, you're losing your touch, luv; I met your 'hook up' last night, and she was fit as, but what did you do, crash out because you can't handle a couple of glasses of Dom', laughed Ritchie, 'but don't worry I made sure she got home safe and got Gregg to drop her off, now get yourself dressed you sad act and I'll treat you to lunch before we head off for the briefing.

The briefing was at fifteen hundred at a location I had yet to be privy to, but at least I would know enough more detail on the 'Dubai job soon' and why there was so much secrecy around what Ritchie was doing.

Gregg dropped us off in Camden, and we went to a small bistro-type place; as we walked in, it was apparent it was a local place' as everyone turned their heads to look us up and down. By the time we had ordered, been served, and eaten, it was half one; Ritchie took a call from someone and then said, 'Gregg will be outside in fifteen. 'we're gonna head straight across to the briefing as it's about an hour drive'. 'No worries, ready when you are', I responded, trying to play it cool, but secretly, I could not wait to discover what was happening.

The journey to the briefing only fuelled my curiosity more. We drove out of central London and headed Southwest on the A3; with my military head on, it didn't take me long to realise we were heading towards Aldershot; again, I wanted to question Ritchie, but I held on thinking an hour, and all will be revealed. We eventually turned off the A3 towards Farnborough and, after about another fifteen minutes pulled into a golf club just North of Farnborough Airfield. 'well, here we are, Lezza, best behaviour please, don't piss anyone off or chat any women up that you like the look of, it's time for us both to put our professional hats on' said Ritchie as he jumped out the car, ' good luck' Gregg said. I couldn't help but notice a sarcastic smirk on his face as I jumped out of the vehicle to follow Ritchie, my heart sank, and I didn't know where to look; I even thought about jumping back in the car and telling Gregg just to drive, but I didn't I just meekly followed Ritchie hoping I wouldn't catch her eye, as I walked into the building thinking what the fuck is going on? Ritchie turned and said, 'Ginny, meet Rach, or you might know her as Becky,' I could feel my face burn up as Rach outstretched her arm to shake my hand. 'Well, Jenny, I mean Ginny, it's a pleasure to meet you again.'

Chapter 5 – 'India, Bravo'

The building the briefing was in reminded me of the D lines in basic training. Even the musty smell was identical; as I walked into a sizeable rectangular-shaped room lined with chairs, I thought, 'What the fuck is going on? Did Ritchie set me up to ensure I didn't get pissed and make a tit out of him, or was it payback for how I treated him with the whole 'Tommy' situation. I couldn't get my head around what it was all about, but when I was in that room, I could feel Rach's eyes burning through the back of my head. I didn't know whether I felt pissed off or embarrassed, but one thing was for sure I'd find out on the long flight to Dubai, as Ritchie had obviously forgotten we were sitting next to each other.

A presentation was being projected onto a white wall, and it was titled 'India Bravo' with the marking TOP SECRET. It all now started to fall into place that this job was not going to be just about looking after some 'rich bitch' as Ritchie had put it; there was much more to it, and I think I was about to find out just how much more there was to the Dubai job.

I glanced around casually but took a mental note of all the personas that were starting to fill the room; the only other female was Rach, and the rest were male and a mixture of what I would describe as your obvious ex-special forces mixed with some nerdy looking IT guys, this was beginning to look a lot like an undercover job with a range of government agencies involved, and I wouldn't say I liked the feel of it. Still, I knew that's exactly why Ritchie hadn't let me in on it; firstly, he probably couldn't even if he had wanted to; secondly, he knew I would have said no straight away as I was done with all the secretive 'sneaky beaky' shit, or so I thought as there was no turning back now. One of the 'ex-special forces' looking guys stood up and walked over to start the briefing; when he put the first slide up, it took every last bit of me not to get up and walk out as I could not believe what I was seeing just on the first paragraph.

The guy presenting introduced himself as Nick and began to repeat pretty much the first paragraph: ' I don't think I need to remind you all what happened in Afghanistan four years ago; for the past two years, we've been tracking a tail 'India Bravo' who we believe is the financial backer of the terrorist group who carried out the attack and continues to finance attacks on coalition forces across the Middle East, your all here to play a part in gathering further intelligence so we can take down this bastard and the terrorist groups he's supporting. I appreciate that up until this point, a few of you in the room thought you were going on a normal 'CP job.' I want you to keep in the back of your mind that you will be protecting some people intricately linked to 'India Bravo', but you have all been chosen because of your previous military roles and credible service. Everything that follows in this briefing may touch nerves amongst you, especially those who have lost comrades because of this bastard, but you all have the credentials needed, so put personal vendettas you may have aside and throw yourself into the role you are playing to become your Clients, confidant, so you can at the right time extract information that will lead us to capture 'India Bravo'. We will issue you an individual brief on your 'Client', and the flight is a private chartered one flown by our sourced pilots so you can read up and prepare to get into the role immediately upon arrival. Those of you who wanted your final 'shag' and woke up this morning thinking, what the fuck happened last night? I can tell you 'Nothing did, we had you drugged, and each person you met, as you may have already seen, is in this room as we could not afford for any of you to go out and chat shit about your 'CP job in Dubai', don't worry it wasn't anything heavy and it will be out of your system by the time we arrive in Dubai, so take note of everything that follows, get focused and prepare to be part of the team that finally gets justice for all those friends, loved ones, comrades we've lost.'

As I was trying to take everything in that had just been said at the same time, I could feel a fire raging in my head, 'What the fuck, Ritchie, you expect me to hold my shit together after this' but Then everything that Nick had said made me realise as I looked around the room, that there were many people who had lost as I could see the same look that was probably on my face which reflected how we were all trying to keep our shit together because we wanted to catch the bastard who had financed the attacks that had taken so many lives from us.

When the briefing finished, I stood up, and Ritchie headed straight toward me; I could see the guilt and concern on his face and before he could apologise, I said, 'Ritchie, I'm okay with this; don't get me wrong I've felt every kind of emotion through that brief, but I'm 110% in, let's get this bastard.

My Intelligence pack was the size of an encyclopaedia; as I settled into the flight, I turned the first page and noticed my 'character name' Sara Rodgers and thought I needed to practice that. I don't know how I hadn't clicked earlier, but it quickly became apparent that Ellen Fatima Shervani was only the daughter of 'India Bravo; I was going to be the closest I would ever get in my life to avenging Jane's death, yet I knew I had to do everything to become Sharvani's best friend so I could feed the team with the intel they need to track her piece of shit father down and bring him to justice.

This was going to be one hell of a job, but I knew from everything I had been through it had brought me to this job. This was my moment to find some closure. Maybe my heart is forever broken, but playing such a big part in catching 'India Bravo' would at least suppress some of the anger and turmoil of losing Jane and give me an opportunity to know that I contributed something that would make her proud of me.

As I read into every detail of Ellen Sharvani's life, I couldn't piece together how she wasn't aware of or even involved with her father's terrorist support; she seemed to be oblivious although she deeply loved her father, and as an only child, after losing her mother in a plane crash when she was young, she only had her father to look up to. I suppose that could make you blinkered.

It was clear that Ellen Sharvani led a secret life that her father had no idea of, and knowing that he was funding terrorists worldwide, I wondered how he would take finding out she was gay. An influential businesswoman who professionally owned her property business selling and renting out modern, high-spec apartments, the brief listed a few of her properties, and when I saw Mexham Gardens was one of her rentals, it all began to make sense, it provided as part of the CP job and not from the 'sneaky beakies'. As I turned the last page of the briefing, an announcement was made to say we were halfway through the flight, so I packed away the brief and thought it the best time to get a bit of sleep before the wheels went down and the start of the takedown of 'India Bravo.'

I was awoken by the sound of the wheels hitting the tarmac. The hitting of the brakes slightly sprung me forward, 'What were you dreaming of, your dribbling?' laughed Ritchie, too, who had been engrossed in his brief. I realised that although he knew more than me, he must have been kept in the dark on the details as I'd never seen him so attentive and quiet. Still, he was always game for a joke on my behalf. As I wiped away a bit of escaped saliva, ' I said your sister Ritchie', whom I had previously 'turned' on a one-night stand, and it always pissed Ritchie off as she was a happily married 'Heterosexual'. 'Fuck off Ginny, what have I told you about mentioning my sister' Ritchie bit. Ritchie had found out in his later years that he had a biological sister whom he never had any idea about; she was a couple of years older and had been searching for Ritchie for years, and low and behold, I only found out after a one night stand with a random, asked Ritchie to pick me up and the look of horror when he realised it was his sister I'd slept with, I found it hilarious, but Ritchie had been fuming.

As the plane pulled into a terminal, it brought back memories of the time Jane and I spent in Dubai after I was shot; I was transferred for treatment in Dubai and Jane, by coincidence, was going on rest and recovery in Dubai, so she spent all of it by my side in the hospital, and that is when we became close and finally a couple. As my thoughts drifted, I could hear her voice saying, 'This is your next journey in life, Ginny; grasp it with both hands. I constantly tried to figure out whether I heard her voice or was just me, hoping to hear her advice and approval again. I had started to cope a bit better since I stopped the heavy drinking, but truth be told, my heart ached for her every day, and I missed her so much.

Ritchie clipped me round the head and said, 'What have I told you? Are you still thinking about my sister? come on shit; lips were getting off the plane.' Walking through Dubai Airport was always like you were in a Super Mall and not much had changed, really; we collected our bags and headed into arrivals as we had been briefed someone would be waiting for us to take us directly to the Sharvani estate as the client wanted to meet us before we booked into our hotels.

I had forgotten to check out which hotel we were staying at, so I asked Ritchie, 'Where are we staying? Anywhere posh?' 'Haven't you read your brief, slacking already? You better sharpen up because you, my dearest friend, on the personal request of Ms Sharvani, are staying in her villa in

Palm Jumeirah as she wants you on hand for a good fingerbang when she's feeling a bit horny', 'you're a dirty bastard Ritchie and remember what you said to me about being in the best form, take your own advice, where are you staying? 'I asked. 'Oh, I'm just slumming it down the road in one of her apartments, he replied.

As we walked into the arrivals lounge, we were greeted almost instantly by what I assumed was Sharvani's entourage; she was pushing the boat out for us. I was approached straight away by a small, geeky-looking woman in her late twenties, 'Ms Rogers, it's very nice to meet you. I'm Ms Sharvani's assistant, Alana, and she wanted me to personally come and greet you and take you to her villa, so please let my colleagues take your bags and let me show you to your vehicle,' she said in a very well-spoken British accent.

I wondered whether she was a plant too as I followed her outside to a very nice but extremely expensive Bugatti Veyron, 'well, this is your ride for the time you are here,' Alana said, trying to be cool, 'my jaw must have hit the ground as I turned to look for Ritchie and he was already looking at the car and mouthed to me 'you jammy bitch'.

Alana drove for the thirty-minute drive to Palm Jumeirah, and I got a full running commentary of how to work all the gadgets; I seriously could not get over the fact that I would be driving around Dubai in a Bugatti for the next few months, then I realised how up, close and personal I was going to be with Shervani. I was committed to discovering what the team needed to know to catch 'India Bravo', but fuck me if she's giving me her Bugatti from the get-go. This girl is going to be a sweetheart. I must keep it together and stay on task; remember why you're here, Ginny, to avenge Jane's death. Finally, I told myself in my head.

'Here we are', 'welcome to Ms Sharvani's residence', we were clearly in the most expensive part of Dubai, and I knew I would be amazed. Still, as we continued through a street of what I can only explain as multi-billionaires' houses, I was blown away; we pulled up to a large electronic gate and then went up to a row of garages, which I presumed were filled with expensive cars.

We pulled into one of the garages, and as the automatic door lifted, I was welcomed by a full-length glass window that led to what looked like a swimming pool and gym.

As we left the garage and headed through a door that led to a sizeable marble-decked hall and staircase, I was just about to turn to Alana to ask if my luggage had followed us. Still, she spoke first as she turned to face up the marble staircase, 'Ms Rogers, please may I introduce you to Ms Sharvani?' As I turned my head and looked up, my stomach did a complete somersault, and for what seemed like an age, no words would come out of my mouth.

I had seen a picture of Elle Sharvani and knew she was beautiful, but seeing her in person was something else; she was stunningly beautiful and had such a kind glow as she smiled at me and said, Alana, 'What have I told you only introduce me as Ms Sharvani to business associates, she then looked deep into my eyes took my hand and said 'Hi Sara, I'm Elle, thank you so much for taking this role it's wonderful to meet you finally'.

Chapter 6 – Elle

I felt like I'd held onto her hand for just that moment too long. As I felt my cheeks start to burn with embarrassment, just at the right time, Elle turned to Alana and said, 'Get Giles to cook something up for Sara'; I'll show her to her room; I almost looked as if to say 'who the fuck is Sara before I told myself to get a grip as it was my cover name. Honestly, Ms Sharvani, I'm fine. You don't need to get me some food, as I was going to wander around, get used to the place, and probably find a pizza shop later. I said, 'Oh please, don't you all Alana on me. She joked, Call me Elle, and for long as you're my BG, you need to get used to not wanting for anything; all my staff are here to feed and water you and if you do want a pizza later, which is an excellent shout by the way, one of them will go and get you the best pizza in town, now come on, let me show you to your room.

As I walked behind Elle up the marble staircase, I didn't know where to look, as her place was out of this world, her arse was the most toned I'd ever seen, and the slim silk Gucci joggers she wore complemented her figure. I nearly choked as she turned and said, 'So, do you like the scenery so far, Sara?', again there was such a kindness about her smile; it was genuine, a bit flirty and sexy; my instinct was telling me to say, ' I love the scenery, walking behind such a fine ass', but my professionality responded, 'What I've seen so far Ms Sharvani, I mean Elle, sorry, is just stunning, you have a lovely home,

'Well, Sara, this is your home too now for the next six months, so please treat it as so; I want you to know I'm not some rich bitch who feeds off Daddy; everything you see here is paid for with my own money, and if I ever piss you off, please do just tell me, I'd like to think we can become friends. I can tell you like to work out as you are in great shape, so

I'm hoping you can put me through my paces.' I was almost sure she was flirting with me. Still, I somehow had adapted to my role as 'Sara' quite well and just responded, 'Yes, sure, it would be great to have a gym buddy; as for putting you through your paces, I think it may be the other way around, I joked. The flirting was confirmed as she stopped suddenly, so much we were almost face to face as she said, 'Oh, I would like that very much.'

We got to a large oak door, and Elle passed me a key and said, 'Right, this is your room, Sara. I'll give you time to settle in. I've no plans for tonight, but if you still want a pizza later on, let me know, and I'll join you. I've got a winery in the basement and what I like to call my 'comfy room,' so if you don't mind me joining, I'll let you pick a bottle, and it's pizza and wine night before we hit the gym tomorrow. 'Sounds great', I responded as I took the key. She also passed me a mobile phone, 'This is yours, and I've put my number in, so drop me a what's an app when you're hungry', and I hope you like your room'. As I walked into the room and turned to close the door, Elle turned and gave a little wave and a smile; I stopped for a moment to catch my breath and took the last twenty minutes in and recoup before I entered the room.

When Elle said room, she was playing it down, or I had no idea how the other half lived; I had what seemed like an entire wing of the first floor of her villa. The bedroom was open plan into a wet room that looked like something straight out of The Real Housewives of Beverly Hills; everything was modern but had a touch of elegance; marble was the 'Dubai' look. I then had a massive hall that led to the kitchen, which again was marble and open plan; it was like a separate house within a house. I couldn't believe this would be my home for the next six months; my jaw dropped even further when I walked into the kitchen and saw large patio doors that were the entire length of one side of the kitchen, which must have been at least four meters, as I walked across and opened the door, I was met with a beautifully lit marble private patio which looked out over the marina, there was a hot tub big enough to fit about eight people in, a small pool and a private sauna, I think the next six months are going to be ok I thought to myself, my thoughts were suddenly interrupted by my phone ringing, as I looked to see it was Ritchie, I switched it to facetime, to show off my new abode as I knew he would be fuming.

'So, how's your digs?' Ritchie asked. I gave him the full virtual tour, showing off my new home for the next six months, 'So come on then, what about Sharvani? Is she fitter in real life? Questioned Ritchie. Before I could hide my emotion, I blurted out, 'She's stunning; she has a real kindness about her.' Ritchie paused and then looked serious for once as he said, 'Remember why we are here, Ginny; I brought you here to get closure by bringing her terrorist funding father to justice so that you can move on; we don't know if she's involved, so by all means your job is to get close so you can extract information, but don't get involved in any other way'.

I played off Ritchie's 'advice' with a sarcastic usual response. Still, when I put the phone down, I had an overwhelming feeling of guilt. I was here to avenge Jane and bring to justice one of the people responsible for her death, yet I was in awe of his daughter. Ritchie was right; I had to get close.

Still, I couldn't start assuming she was kind and friendly; just because she gave me an expensive car and home to live in, I could have been anyone, so this is how she would have treated anyone who had ended up as her BG.

I looked at my watch; it was just past seven p.m. It was still hot outside, and I thought, what better time to try out the pool and Sauna? I went back into the bedroom, suddenly realising that I hadn't seen my luggage arrive and hadn't packed any swimwear, as it hadn't crossed my mind that I would have my own private pool, hot tub and sauna. There were primarily mirrored built-in wardrobes, so I thought, 'fuck it, it's a private area, and unless someone is on the other side of the marina with top-notch binos, no one's going to see me starkers', I opened the wardrobe hoping to grab a towel and low and behold, Elle had thought of everything as hanging up was a variety of swim wear, which included bikini's, swimming costumes and swim shorts and vests, all top designer names like Gucci, Fendi, Versace and strangely they were all my size, as I decided which one I would sport, the phone Elle had given me rang so I answered, 'Hi Sara, sorry to disturb you, it's just I assumed that you wouldn't have brought any swimwear so there's a few options for you in the wardrobe, I hope I got the right size, laughed Elle, 'yes I've just spotted them as I thought I would go for a quick dip before ordering a pizza, thank you, they are the perfect size, but, you didn't have to do that 'I replied. 'Well, great, I am glad I got the right size; enjoy your swim, and I will see you for pizza later. Said Elle, 'Yes, sure, I'll be about an hour,' I responded, then said goodbye and headed for the pool.

It was around nine pm by the time I went down to Elle's 'comfy room', which was a massive underestimation of the room; it was like a cinema, a large screen at the front on a wall that must have towered about 10ft, there was a built-in neon-lit hot tub and a combination of king-size beanbags and sofas, there was a bar in the far corner which was already lined with a variety of pizzas.

'How was your swim?' asked Elle, 'Great,' I replied thanks again for the swimwear.' 'No problem at all, now come and pick a nice bottle to wash down our pizza,' said Elle, gesturing to me to follow her. We made our way down into a private basement that was indeed a winery and must have been the total size of the room above; it was layered with bottle racks containing various wines. I wouldn't have usually engaged straight away in alcohol consumption with a client. Still, my brief was to get close as quickly as possible and say yes to every social gathering or event offer, so I guess this was within my remit.

I had no idea when it came to wine other than picking the most expensive, hoping it meant it was the nicest; as I was shown around the racks of wine and given a complete description of each one, I had to admit my lack of knowledge.

'Elle, I have to be honest. I usually go for the most expensive one, hoping it will taste as good as it costs, so I'm totally out of my depth here, I joked.

'Well, let's test that theory then, Sara', my father got me this and boasted about it being the most expensive in the world, so let's see what it tastes like, as I've never fancied having it on my own' said Elle, as she picked up a bottle of red wine called La Tache.

The first mention of her Father stirred a bit of deep, routed anger in me, but I also noticed that her face changed as she mentioned her father. I sensed a little resentment in her tone and delinquency that drinking it would piss her father off, I had no idea what kind of 'expense' this bottle of red was, but if it meant it would piss her father off, I was one hundred and ten per cent up for drinking it.

Elle poured us a glass each, and as I took a sip, it tasted like red wine, 'So what's the verdict, Sara? Does the expense match the taste' questioned Elle, 'Well, I have to be honest again, Elle, it just tastes like red wine', but yeah, it's palatable, so if you don't mind me asking, how expensive is it, I'm guessing a couple of hundred quid?' I guessed. Elle giggled and said, 'It's about four thousand pounds for a bottle'. I nearly spat the mouthful of wine I had just taken everywhere as I said, 'You're shitting me, four grand for a bottle of wine.'

As we started on the second bottle of red, I felt I was getting tipsy and knew I couldn't get too pissed. Elle had said the only plans we had for tomorrow were the gym and dinner with a business associate in the evening she was hosting in her villa, so she didn't need me to be around, as her residential security team would be in. Alana would show me a private club she liked to attend, as she had plans to go there at the weekend, so it would be a good opportunity for me to look around and get Alana to show me her regular haunts.

She also briefly mentioned lunch with her father on Friday as he was taking a business trip away for the weekend and wanted to see her before he went, so I had to get used to the idea that sooner or later, I would come face to face with the person responsible for taking away the love of my life.

I noticed that Elle was getting tipsier, and when she went to get a third bottle, I knew I had to keep a level head as much as possible. The problem was you could not help but take to this stunning and kind woman; she was enchanting, and as she topped up my glass, smiling at me as she poured the wine, I didn't refuse, and to be fair, it was starting to taste more and more like a four-grand bottle of red.

I checked my watch and could not believe it was midnight; it was the right time to call it a night as my head was almost spinning, and the third bottle was practically empty.

'Elle, thank you for such a lovely evening, but I think I need some beauty sleep before our gym session tomorrow,' I suggested. Elle leaned in close to me, looked me straight in the eye and flirted, 'Oh Sara, you don't need beauty sleep; you're a naturally beautiful-looking woman. However, I'm slightly drunk, and before I embarrass myself, I will bid you goodnight and thank you for your excellent company. And I hope we will continue to get to know each other personally over the next few months as she kissed me on each cheek and said goodnight.

I returned to my room and lay on my bed, thinking of everything that had happened on my first night with Elle. I could not hide away from the fact that I felt a natural connection with her, and my head and heart would be in a constant battle for the next six months because I had to ensure I remained focused on the task at hand. I procrastinated; yes, she appeared kind, stunning and flirted with me, but the realisation hit hard. This was the woman whose father had played a significant part in Jane's death, my soulmate, my true love.

I didn't know her or what she was capable of herself, and as I drifted off to sleep, my head heavy with the consumption of three bottles of costly red wine, my heart also started to feel heavy with the loss of the woman I had only ever truly loved.

Chapter 7 – The Plane Crash

I woke up feeling surprisingly fresh, as I had expected a lousy head after consuming much more alcohol than I had intended, but I felt okay. Nothing a cold shower and a coffee would not sort out before hitting the gym with Elle.

I was looking forward to getting out in the afternoon and doing a few recces on Elle's regular haunts and business premises, and it also allowed me to get out in my new flash wheels. I had arranged to meet Elle at zero nine thirty in the gardens, and the plan was to head to her gym, which I'd yet to see but was on her estate, so I assumed it wasn't far. I wore shorts and a

T-shirt as the Dubai heat was so dry, and I knew working out would be very sweaty.

    As I made my way into the gardens, Elle was already there on a call on her mobile phone. She turned, gestured that she wouldn't be long, and gave me another one of those flirty smiles.

I could faintly make out that she had said father a couple of times and noticed that there was sarcasm in her tone, and it made me wonder about her relationship with her father. Did she know what he was involved in? Or didn't she know that her father was a murdering scumbag?

Elle was genuine and sincere and didn't have a bad bone in her body, but how couldn't she know about her father? He had brought her up, having lost her mum at age ten. It was in the briefing pack that her mother had been on a private flight from Iran after visiting on business which crashed; her body or the plane wreckage had never been found, but all on board were presumed dead, which included her mother, her mother's assistant, the pilot and three onboard staff.

It must have been hard for Elle, losing her mother so young and being brought up by her father, but I assumed that their bond would be substantial, having gone through losing her mother and his wife together.

'Sorry about that, Sara. Shall we head across? I'm looking forward to you putting me through my paces, and also, I know you like boxing, so I think you'll be impressed with the new kit I've put into the gym,' smiled Elle. How did she know I liked boxing? I thought for a split second, but then it had probably been on my CV that Ritchie would have submitted, so I brushed it off.

Elle wasn't lying when she said I'd be impressed; as we walked into her gym, it was like walking into a top-of-the-range gym. There were two floors, and the bottom floor was like a boxing gym. It had a ring, six bags, lots of free weights, and jump boxes. It was like she knew my workout routine, as every piece of equipment I would usually use was in her gym.

'So, what do you think, Sara?' said Elle smugly, 'Wow, it's amazing, Elle,' let's get to work, I replied.

We had been working out for about an hour when Elle said, 'Right, come on then, Sara, I want to see your boxing skills; let's get in the ring and spar.', 'Are you sure? I don't want to be sacked on day two for giving you a shiner,' I joked, 'I like your confidence, but don't underestimate me, Sara; I've been in the ring a couple of times before, let me tell you 'She joked back.

We wore gloves and a head guard and set the clock for three two-minute rounds. I started the first round, throwing a few soft jabs, conscious not to hurt Elle; Elle moved well around the ring and had some excellent footwork, which made me think she had done this before. Just as I was in mid-thought, I felt a straight jab to the nose, waking me up and thinking, Right, let's spar then.

We were having a good little move around, and I was impressed with Elle's sparring; she was probably eight stone wet through, but she could punch. It reminded me of the sparring I used to do back home in an ex-pro boxers' gym where a few girls were involved in the white-collar scene. I had immediately wanted to get involved, and between us, we would punch the shit out of each other when sparring and then laugh about it in a bar afterwards.

Elle must have noticed my concentration slip again as I reminisced, and she connected well with my solar plexus, taking the wind out of my sails and making me drop to my knees. As I sucked in air, I was so embarrassed; Elle threw her gloves off and came and knelt beside me, 'Sara, I'm so sorry, but I did warn you not to underestimate me she joked. I don't know what hurt me more; the punch or my pride at the person I was supposed to be a bodyguard for had just put me on my ass. 'Let me have a look and make sure I didn't break a rib; she joked as she pulled my T-shirt up slightly, and then her face changed as she noticed the scar I had on my abdomen from being shot in Afghanistan. Elle paused awkwardly momentarily as she let go of my T-shirt and said, 'Do you mind telling me what happened?' 'Oh, this little scratch was from when I served in the forces,' I said casually, 'did you get shot?' Elle asked with such a show of concern on her face.

'Yeah, I'm the one who scares the living daylight out of kids when they ask if you have ever been shot,' I joked. Elle moved her hand to my abdomen and brushed her fingers over my scar as she said, 'I'm sorry that happened to you, Sara.' It looks like it was nasty, and you're lucky to be here,' said Elle. Jane's words came to mind, and I said, 'Oh, don't worry, my abs saved me. As you can see, I've got a bit of a washboard,' I joked back.

'Well, they didn't stop my punch to your solar plexus, did they?' Elle laughed as she reached out her hand to help me up. 'Let me take you out for lunch tomorrow to make up for it; I won't take no

for an answer,' Asked Elle, 'Ok, sounds good,' I
replied.

I couldn't deny at that moment that she had run her
fingers over my scar. It had sent butterflies through
my body; something about Elle was captivating. She
seemed honest and genuinely caring, and I could see
the hurt in her eyes as she felt my scar. Again, I had
to battle my emotions; I was sure this woman was
flirting with me, and I admittedly was also flirting
back. I had to get my head straight and focus; it was
only day two, yet I felt like I had known Elle for so
much longer.

I spent the afternoon driving around Elle's local
haunts and business locations with Alana, getting to
know routes and business associates as although it
had been an easy ride up until now, Elle's schedule

was mad busy starting from next week, and for once, I focused on doing a good job. I could feel the 'old me' was back in business and back in the game.

Alana had pre-stored all of Elle's known locations, and as we had stopped for a quick brew, I flicked through the sat nav to the following place, which was just titled 'Maria'. Before I could ask, Alana spoke and looked at me seriously. 'Oh, this one is Ms Sharvani's acquaintance, and you need to ensure that you don't mention any visits to anyone as the strictest confidence is required of you, Sara. It would be best if you did not mention Ms. Sharvani's visits to anyone, not even her father. Is that clear? 'Yes, understood loud and clear, Alana, you have my word,' I replied, but what did I feel? A pang of jealousy? Was this Elle's girlfriend, and did she not want her father to know or get arrested? I hated when people told me things like this, as I was again intrigued and wondered whether Elle would eventually tell me. But for now, I felt slightly jealous and thought, " Right, that's it, Ginny, stop the flirting now and remember what this job is all about.

The weeks passed, and before I knew we were halfway through the job, I'd grown extremely close to Elle and had, on occasion, nearly forgotten about the real reason I was there and just got on with the job. We had made numerous trips to 'Maria', and I never got to see who she was. It was the one thing that Elle would never chat to me about, as she did with all her other business meetings or socials, and I was starting to think that this was either a long-term 'fuck buddy' or her girlfriend. It was funny as whenever Elle got into the car after a 'Maria' visit, she always looked at me with a look of guilt, and I assumed that was because she fancied the pants off me and felt guilty it wasn't me; she was fucking.

As I sat waiting outside a lovely block of apartments waiting for Elle to return after another visit to 'Maria', I started to think about the task I had ahead of me in the evening; tonight was the first night I would be in the same room as her father, and I had got so anxious about how I would react the first time I saw the person who played a part in the death of my soulmate. It was taking everything I had to remain professional.

As my thoughts drifted towards Jane for the first time in a few weeks, as I had been so busy, I noticed that Elle was in the foyer of the building. Alana hugged her as if she was upset; I immediately jumped out of the car. However, remembering my clear instructions never to approach or enter the building, I awkwardly put my thumb up to Alana to signal if everything was okay. Immediately, my phone rang; it was Alana. Sara, could you get back in the car? Ms Sharvani is fine, and we will be across in five minutes, 'Yes, sure, I replied; I just wanted to check you were both ok?'. 'We are fine, as I said and will be with you shortly,' Alana said abruptly before hanging up.

A lover's tiff, I thought. But in the three months I had been here, I had never seen Elle upset, and as I got back into the car, I could see that she was in some state; her shoulders were shaking like someone does when they are sobbing uncontrollably. She must have liked this woman, I thought.

From my experiences, I learned that the worst thing to do when someone is upset and has fully regained themselves is to ask if they are okay. So, when Elle returned to the car without a streak of make-up or any indication that she had been upset, I just acknowledged her return as I had always done after any meeting or social, with a cheery 'ready to go?'

'Yes, thank you, Sara, Elle replied, but as I caught her eye, she looked deep into mine and said with a serious tone and slight callous smile, 'I'm more than ready.' What did that mean, I thought, but assumed again it was down to what was now a broken relationship and the last time I would take her to see 'Maria.'

As we drove back to the house, there was a different feeling in the air, and Elle hardly spoke, which was not like her at all; I tried to make my usual chat as we drove but soon realised she was somewhere else, and for a moment it reminded me of what I was probably like when I lost Jane, vacant, heartbroken and not wanting to communicate with anyone, so I left her to her thoughts.

As we pulled into her estate, I tried to initiate a final conversation and said, 'So Elle, are we still leaving for your fathers at seven pm? Elle's head spun around as if I had just slapped her across the face, and I felt momentarily that she would have said something different as she paused and said, 'Yes, please, Sara, that would be great.'

Amir Sharvani had a private estate in the Emirate Hills; I had recce'd the route and estate the day before and, for the first time in three months, had a very brief catch-up with Ritchie, who was also taking his client to the 'Family gathering' that was occurring tonight, Ritchie had told me he was staying in an apartment in 'Downtown Dubai' looking after the son of Amir from a second marriage. It was unusual for Ritchie; he hadn't gone into too much detail, but we only had a quick five minutes together, so I just put it down to that, and we would have a more extended catch-up tonight whilst the family ate.

I picked Elle up as planned at seven pm, and I must admit she looked terrific and felt that she had put in an extra effort, maybe trying to seduce me. It was more likely down to how you react to a breakup to make yourself feel better.

I hadn't meant to stare just that little bit longer. I hadn't planned on speaking out loud when I blurted out, ' Wow, Elle, you look stunning.' I could feel the heat in my cheeks immediately as I blushed with pure embarrassment; Elle responded by putting her hand on my leg and leant in towards me and kissing me on the cheek as she playfully said, 'Hopefully that will cool your cheeks'.

I didn't know what to do or say, and my actions were uncontrollable; I turned my head towards Elle, who was still facing me, and without intending to, our lips locked, and that was it; we had our first kiss. The natural connection between us had gotten the better of us; as we closed in an embrace and kissed passionately, I could feel her hands wandering up to my breast, and as much as I wanted her, I knew in a split moment I had to stop.

I grasped her hand, held it, pulled gently away and said, 'Elle, we can't do this. Her reply made me laugh aloud. 'We can, Sara, but maybe not now; we can continue this later, maybe,' she smiled as she pulled her hand away and checked herself in the mirror.

You would have thought that the journey to Elle's father's estate would have been awkward after 'the kiss', but it wasn't. We chatted and laughed as we always did, and I couldn't help feeling something for this woman who sat next to me. I wasn't sure what it was, but I knew it felt like something I thought I would never feel again since losing Jane.

I knew I had overstepped the line, and I honestly can't tell you how it happened other than that as two people, we had a connection and foolishly acted upon that connection. I knew I had to have a talk with Elle and stop it going any further, but for now, I had to snap back to reality as we were pulling into the driveway of her father's estate, and I was about to come face to face for the first time with her father.

I had never seen such a lineup of expensive cars as we pulled up at the front of the main house. Also, I had never seen so many BGs in one place simultaneously, and I was slightly perplexed to see that the security on the estate was all armed, obviously due to Amir Sharvani's 'status'. As I got out and opened the door for Elle, she smiled and said, 'I'll come and find you later, Sara; I'd like you to meet my father. He will love you, and I want to ensure he tips you well.

I assumed she liked to tease her father with her sexuality, and I would be a good pawn for her to do so; I nodded and replied, 'I'd love to, and then, under my breath, muttered, kill him'.

As a porter approached to park the car and direct me to a separate building, I saw Ritchie, and he waved me over. As I walked across, I noticed he had a serious look on his face, and I immediately knew something was wrong. 'Sara, how are you? It's nice to see you,' said Ritchie; his professionalism and tone threw me, and I nearly called him Ritchie for a second. Instead, I gathered myself and replied,

'John, I'm well, thank you. How are you?' This whole situation was strange, but regardless, I carried it on whilst we were still in earshot of the porters.

Ritchie led me to a building which looked like a garage. He hadn't said a word, and I just had that horrible gut feeling in my stomach. For a moment, I thought back to 'the kiss' in the car and wondered whether the car was bugged and he was pissed off I'd broken the golden rule on such a big job, but as I walked into the building, I realised straight away that this little gathering was for a reason a lot more severe than a little kiss.

In the room were all the same personalities as in the pre-deployment brief. For a moment, I thought seriously, we will talk business here, whilst the

number one target is eating dinner with his family
one hundred yards away.

A guy called 'Slim' almost read my mind and said,
'Quick search, guys and girls, and all mobile phones
switched off, we have a comms blocker within 10
yards of this building, so we just need to check none
of you have been bugged, he then looked me straight
in the eye and joked ' you lucky bitch, snogging the
face off Sharvani's daughter, great move though
you've got her in deep now'.

I looked to Ritchie with my 'what the fuck'
expression, and he laughed and said, 'Come on
Ginny, surely you knew we had to bug the car for

your safety more than anything, but I agree, well played, you are playing the exact part we brought you here to do'. At that moment, it all suddenly clicked. I was supposed to 'get close' to Elle as part of bringing down her father, and Ritchie knew I would get involved. 'You fucking prick, Ritchie, you have pimped me out, I joked, but deep down, I hadn't planned this, and I certainly didn't want to play Elle; she wasn't her father, and I felt like I was deceiving her.

I quickly snapped back to it as Ritchie explained we had about thirty minutes to get an update on the job's progress, and the building had been locked down for free speech with the latest hi-tech comms blocking equipment. I thought it was risky being on her father's estate and all, but equally, I knew how good these guys were, and a job like this always came with risks that must be taken. As I grabbed a cup of coffee and took a seat, I nearly spat my first mouthful everywhere as a presentation was projected onto the white walls of the garage titled 'Maria.'

The same guy who delivered the brief before deployment started to speak:

'Maria is one of our undercover operatives acting as a private investigator for Subject Two (Elle). Subject two has been suspicious about her father's involvement in her mother's death and believes he arranged for an engine fault on the aircraft to get rid of his wife, who had discovered his involvement in financing terrorism.

'Maria' has been in place for almost two years gathering evidence on behalf of Subject Two and has gained her complete trust and built a strong friendship; today, she presented Subject Two with pictures of her stepbrother Omar (Ritchie's client) giving the Pilot who was the only survivor of the crash a large amount of money, so it has confirmed her father's involvement. As you can imagine, she's a bit pissed off.

But as planned, she has fallen straight into the arms or the lips of our lesbian Lothario 'Sara.' Can we all show Sara some appreciation, you lucky bitch,' I could have died of embarrassment on the spot as everyone applauded me, and to hide my feelings, I stood up. I bowed to acknowledge my efforts and continued the banter only military and ex-military share.

He then continued to talk about the next phase of the operation, which would be for me to get close enough to Elle to confide in me what she knew about her father so that the case could be built against him. When the brief finished, I felt I was betraying Elle, and as Ritchie pulled me to one side, I knew what was coming next.

'Ginny, I want to ensure you are okay with all this. I know I've pimped you out a bit, but I knew you would nail this job. He joked but still maintained an air of seriousness. It took everything for me to respond, 'Come on, Ritchie, if you're telling me I get to bag a stunning rich bitch as part of an all-expenses trip to Dubai, then I'm in one hundred and ten per cent, but just to be clear, how far do you want me to go?' 'Oh Ginny, all the fucking way, and do me a favour, for my personal use, record that shit, will ya,' said Ritchie excitedly. 'Fuck off, ya perv, as if that wouldn't look sus; you just leave me to it, and I'll tell you all about it for your imagination,' I joked back. Suddenly, Ritchie adopted a serious tone as he touched my shoulder and said, 'Seriously though, Ginny, you are not catching any real feelings, are you? This must be strictly business, yeah? I wish I hadn't, but I paused for a split second and then said, 'Strictly business pal,' At that moment, I knew Ritchie sensed my guilt, but luckily, a guy from his team approached and said, 'Right time to move,' before he could press any further.

Chapter 8 – Falling.

As I waited in the lounge of Elle's father's mansion, I had a million thoughts running through my mind. It all made sense now, 'Maria', the secrecy. Elle had been investigating her father's involvement in her mother's death, and today, when I had seen her upset, it had been confirmed. Then I thought about the kiss we shared and how it had sent an electric shock through my body, one I thought I would never feel again since I lost Jane, what was I doing and more importantly, how can I get my head straight and focus on the actual job I was here to do.

I quickly snapped out of it as I saw Elle approaching with a big smile. She said, 'Right you, let's get that tip off my so-called father' again, another lapse in her feelings, which made me feel even more guilty as she was beginning to trust and confide in me. Behind Elle was an entourage of burly Middle Eastern men, and in the midst, I caught my first glimpse of Amir Sharvani. He was not what I expected him to look like, as I knew how evil this man was. Yet, he had such a kind and gentle appearance and must have been about 5'2, bald and of an average build; as he approached me, surprisingly, he held out his hand, and as I offered mine, he placed a gentle kiss on my hand and said, 'Sara I believe you are taking outstanding care of my daughter and she speaks extremely highly of you, so please as a token of my utmost appreciation take this gift and thank you for doing a highly professional job of protecting my princess. He handed me a box and an envelope, and remaining professional, I thanked him and placed them in my pocket when I wanted to throw them back in his face.

'I have also arranged for you to have the evening off and join me, Elle, and my son Omar, as well as some of your fellow security team, for some food and drinks and my Security Team will take over from here and ensure you get back home later on.

The invitation caught me off guard as I wasn't expecting it and wasn't sure what was going on and as I looked at Elle, it was almost like she read my

mind and said jokingly, 'Don't worry, Sara, you're

in safe hands, let's have some fun at the expense of

my Father', I looked across to her father who just

smiled proudly back at Elle. It made me wonder

again how he could be so evil yet come across as

kind and gentle.

As we walked through his house, built from top to

bottom of what I can only describe as costly marble,

I took every inch of the house in, feeling slightly

uneasy in the home of such a callous and conspiring

man. As we walked into a large lounge area with a

bar the entire length of one side of the room and a

raised marble structured hot tub, I thought, what the

fuck am I supposed to do here?

Within seconds of walking into the room, I heard

laughter behind me and turned to see Ritchie and a

couple of the guys from the team accompanying

Omar Sharvani into the room; I caught Ritchie's eye.

I could tell he immediately saw the 'what the fuck'

expression on my face, and he gave me a reassuring

smile, which made me feel a little bit more

comfortable and the fact that he and the team had

also been given the invite.

'Right then, attention please, bellowed Mr Sharvani.

Let us get some quick formalities out the way, and

then I want you ladies and gentlemen to enjoy

yourselves. I want to thank you all personally for

protecting my beloved Daughter and Son, and I hope

you all like your gifts.

I know you like to work hard and play even harder,

so tonight is your opportunity to do just that.

The bar and my hospitality team are at your service,

and I have had my team go out and get you all

swimming attire should you wish to use the

facilities. Please relax and have some fun, and I hope to see you all again soon.'

Elle approached me at the end of her father's speech and said she would talk with her brother Omar, then she would be back, so I grabbed a G&T and headed towards Ritchie. As I approached him, he acknowledged me with a smile and 'Hello Sara, how are you enjoying Dubai?' so I played along with general chat until the coast was clear. We were out of earshot of Mr Sharvani's staff and whispered, 'What is going on? Are we doing this tonight? 'Of course, we are just enjoying ourselves, Sara; it will be your only opportunity and keep on doing a fantastic job 'looking after' Ms Sharvani, he replied with a wink and a smile.

About an hour passed until Elle returned, and I could tell that she had been upset and seemed pretty drunk;

she looked at me and gestured me over to her, 'So Sara, my father has left to attend a business meeting, so let me give you a tour of the house? 'Ok, sounds great', I replied, wanting to say, 'Is that a good idea?'

Elle led me out of the lounge, and we headed down to the lower floor; we passed numerous Sharvani's Security Team members, who just bowed with respect as Elle walked past them. 'I want to show you the true beauty of this house, which is the wine cellar and spa', and I have asked my Father's maid to have some swimming attire ready for us so we don't have to flaunt ourselves in front of the rest of the security team', gestured Elle as she held a large Oak door open for me, 'after you, I replied reaching for the door, 'Oh Sara, relax and let me look after you tonight please and remember who dropped you in the boxing gym the other day, you wouldn't want the rest of your team to learn about that, would you? She joked, 'That was a one.' I joked back, 'Wait until next time?' I laughed.

As we entered a long brick corridor, I guessed that this was the wine cellar as there was a line of shelves on each side of the aisle, every metre or so lined with what I could only imagine was costly wine, 'Right, I'm making a calculated guess Sara, that you're a Pinot Grigio type of girl, would that be right?' 'It would indeed', I responded again, knowing that drinking wine was not a clever idea, but I thought ', oh fuck it, I'm going to enjoy myself, just a little.

Elle grabbed two bottles of Pinot Grigio and gestured me to follow as she said, 'Right then, we have vino. Let's slip into something a bit more comfortable, and she walked through another set of double oak doors into a blacked-out room with a pool, jacuzzi and hot tub surrounded by sizeable oval lounge areas with drapes and cushions; this was a different world I thought.

Laid out on one of the lounge beds was a set of matching bikinis, robes and slippers; Elle held them up and laughed, 'Aww, Mary, my father's maid, has got us matching outfits to chill in; how sweet of her and you can't refuse now she's gone to all that effort'. Elle began to get undressed, and I knew she was more than tipsy and honestly wanted the floor to swallow me up as I didn't know where to look. 'Oh, don't be a prude, Sara, come on, get changed; I promise I won't look,' said Elle playfully. Before I knew it, I was bikini-clad and entering the Jacuzzi with a glass of wine.

I looked over at Elle, and for what seemed like an hour but was probably only a minute, I didn't know what to say; Elle just stared back with that captivating and flirtatious smile and then said, 'So, do you want to finish off what we started in the car?'. A thousand things flashed through my mind: Jane, the briefing, her father, the real reason I was here. Elle didn't waste any time, and as she waded towards me through the bubbling water, she said, 'You're a deep thinker, Sara, aren't you? Just relax, and I think this is mutual, so let's have some fun.'

'What about your father or his Security or Maid? What if they come in?' I said nervously, 'Oh, chill out. They are under strict instruction to leave us to have a 'girly night' and won't come anywhere near, and my father's gone to a business meeting, so trust me, it's just you and me,' Elle responded as she reached out a hand and placed it around my neck and pulled me towards her.

Our lips met once again, and it immediately sent shivers down my spine; Elle's lips felt so soft, and I could taste the sweet taste of wine as she passionately placed her tongue inside my mouth. This time, I reached for Elle's breast, caught up in a passionate embrace, and gasped uncontrollably as Elle started to circle my nipples with her finger. Elle moved her mouth down to my breasts and began to circle my nipples with her tongue; I could feel a rush of endorphins, and the throbbing in between my legs was almost uncontrollable as Elle slid her fingers under my bikini briefs. As her hand manoeuvred between my legs and met my vulva, the pulsations from my clitoris were uncontrollable as she continued to suck and caress my nipple with her tongue. There was no doubt that Elle was very experienced in making love to another woman.

I wanted to take control and pleasure Elle. Still, she was in the driving seat. I had experienced many sexual encounters with women but never experienced the joy I was sharing with Elle. I had the most mind-blowing orgasm that women will only know can come from another woman, and it seemed like it would never end. My head was engulfed in fuzziness from continuously climaxing, and as she entered her fingers inside me, my body just gave in to the extreme pleasure.

I finally got the opportunity to return the favour, and I lifted Elle onto the side of the jacuzzi and started to kiss her stomach, making my way down her body to her toes; I placed each toe in my mouth, and she leant her body back with pleasure, I then made my way back up her legs to her inner thigh and teased her with kisses getting close enough to her vulva until the point she guided my head towards her vagina and I kissed her gently across each part of her and then caressed her clitoris with my tongue. After the first climax, I entered her with my tongue, and she loudly moaned as she continued to orgasm.

We embraced each other momentarily and giggled like naughty schoolchildren who could be caught kissing behind the bike sheds at any moment. We climbed out of the jacuzzi and lay on one of the beds in our robes, and the utter fuzziness I was feeling at that moment felt like I was falling for this woman, or was it just that I had had the most fantastic sex?

Within minutes of lying on the bed, we were naked and making love again; this time, we faced each other intensely as we moved our fingers inside each other and kissed passionately. I swear I felt like my head would explode as Elle made me come repeatedly until we both had nothing left and lay together, entwining our bodies.

Elle threw a blanket over me and headed for another couple of bottles of wine.

As Elle fetched more wine, I asked myself again, 'What am I doing?' am I playing the part I've been asked to play, or do I feel something for this woman? As Elle walked back in and looked at me, she looked so stunningly beautiful, and it took my breath away, and I knew it was the latter.

It was almost zero three-thirty by the time we were dropped back at Elle's by her father's security team. As we walked in, clear of the security team, Elle grabbed me by the arm, kissed me on the lips and said, ' I enjoyed tonight with you, Sara and I want you to know that I have been waiting three months to make love to you like we did tonight, as from the moment I set eyes on you I felt something between us, and I know you are here on a professional basis, but I hope that tonight means we can also get to know each other a lot better on a personal basis, if you know what I mean. I didn't have control of the words that came out of my mouth next: ' Elle, I feel the same'. As we walked up the stairs and Elle threw me one last flirtatious glance, I got that same fuzzy feeling, and I knew that I had gone too far and was falling.

In the following weeks, I grew closer to Elle, and we spent more time chatting over lunch, sneaking up into her room on a night; it was the first time since losing Jane that I finally felt I could move on and be happy. So, I just went with my gut feelings. I was a star pupil as far as the task was concerned as Elle was starting to confide in me, and on many occasions, as we lay in bed after another marathon session of lovemaking, she often said, 'Sara, there is so much I want to tell you, but then before I could probe further, we would be making love again.

I constantly battled with my emotions of guilt and betrayal. I had to remind myself every time I nearly said, 'Elle, there's so much I want to tell you too,' why I was here. Then, whatever followed this task was over, I constantly kidded myself that I could tell Elle everything as her hatred for her father must have been on the same level as mine, only she hid it so well.

It dawned on me how her father had come across as a kind and gentle man. Yet, he was capable of the vilest acts of terrorism and arranging the death of his wife, and I would often think to myself, 'Hang on a minute, Ginny, Is Elle playing you, and is she just like her father? It was a constant rollercoaster of

emotions, and I knew deep down that this would not

end well, but I couldn't throw away my second

chance of happiness and, dare I say it, Love.

**Chapter 9 – The Truth, The Whole Truth and
Nothing but the Truth**

As the weeks passed by and the end of the task got nearer, it started to sink in that I was falling in love with Elle, and I had no idea what to do about it. We shared a natural connection; each day we spent time together, I felt she was on the brink of telling me everything.

I hadn't seen Ritchie for a couple of weeks, which I was glad of as I knew he would read me like a book and see that I was falling for Elle. If he knew, he would have no choice but to spill the beans as, ultimately, the job would be compromised. I hoped that time would continue to pass, and I could extract the information on Mr Sharvani from Elle and then pick up with her after the task ended, but who was I kidding as it would never be that simple.

My heart sank as my phone rang, and I knew it was Ritchie; his tone immediately told me something was wrong, but surely, he couldn't have picked up on anything as I had avoided being in his company like the plague. 'Sara, can you make yourself available tonight as there's a 'briefing' on a family event we need you at?' said Ritchie; very matter of fact, I knew this was a code for a serious issue to be discussed and I shit myself thinking I'm just going to have to come clean. 'Yeah, sure, I'll clear it with Elle, er Ms Shavani (shit too personal); what time do you need me and where?' I responded keenly, 'Don't worry about the location; someone from the team will pick you up (again, a red flag). Just be ready for about eighteen thirty, and just like that, Ritchie hung up.

I knew that by the abruptness and short call, a shit storm would descend, and I felt I would be right in the middle of it.

Just as I was about to leave my room and speak to Alana to see if I could be excused for a couple of hours, I bumped straight into her in the hallway, and before I could ask, she said, ' Sara, Ms Sharvani would like to see you please about an event she would like to attend'. Alana sounded off, and I wouldn't say I liked her tone. As I replied, 'Sure', she said, follow me and didn't engage in the usual casual chit-chat.

I started feeling freaked out and knew I had to get a grip on myself. As I followed Alana, we headed towards the garages at the back of the estate, and I realised I had never actually been to them before. I wondered why we were going there now; I felt intrigued yet slightly concerned as we approached. I asked Alana, 'Are we going out in one of Ms Sharvani's cars?' Alana responded firmly, 'Just follow me, Sarah; you will know everything shortly.' What did she mean? 'Know everything?

At this point, I could feel that I was starting to lose my shit, and it was taking every ounce of me to remain calm; as we entered the garage, Alana led me to an oak wall, removed a book and just when I was about to say 'what the fuck is that for' the wall rotated and made way to what I could only assume was a hidden room. There stood in the doorway, and Elle smiled at me with the warmest, most loving smile.

I was vexed to the max, and as she gestured me in, I walked towards her as the wall rotated back into place with Alana on the opposite side; I looked to my left. It confirmed that a shit storm was en route, if not imminent, and I was in the middle.

The room was made from solid stone with a fake oak wall on the entry point from the garage, obviously to hide its location. I could tell from my days carrying out 'special ops' that it was intentionally built this way to be safe for internal communications, and it reminded me of interrogation training. As my thoughts of 'why am I here?', is this the honest Elle, and are my dark thoughts of Elle being just like her father right? Filling my mind, I looked back to the wall that had caught my attention immediately on the left as I walked in. It was covered from bottom to top in a whiteboard with pictures, a map and notes, and I just knew this was a moment of the truth unfolding.

Elle walked towards me and held her hands, arms fully extended. I felt slightly uneasy, but her gaze and smile told me this would be her revelation, not mine. I gazed back at her lovingly, trapped by my own heart and ever-increasing love for this woman and held out my hands to hold hers; I almost missed it as she said, 'Ginny, don't be worried, it's ok; I'm going to tell you exactly why you are here', sheer panic filled my body, and as she held tightly onto my hands, I felt my whole body freeze. As I attempted to respond with 'Who's

Ginny? What are you talking about? I glanced beyond Elle and fixed my eyes on the whiteboard to discover what might come next. What I saw, I was never expecting, and as everything went hazy for a moment, I wasn't sure whether I had fainted or been struck by something, but all I could see was a picture clear as anything, a picture of Jane.

I came back to my senses slowly as the haze cleared, and over me knelt Elle, with a worried expression as she dabbed my forehead with a flannel, 'Ginny, you fainted. Are you ok? I'm so sorry that it's come to this, but please let me explain. I don't care what your name is, I need you to know this: above everything else, I will tell you, 'I love you'. I tried to speak and get up to piece everything together and establish if this was real and if I wasn't having a bad dream. Elle gently held me down and said, 'Take it easy, get up slowly, or you will end up fainting again; I've so much to tell you, but we don't have too much time'.

There was no point in pretending to be Sara anymore. As much as my head told me not to divulge in a conversation, my heart led to my response, 'Elle, I promise you it was never my intention to fall in love with you, and for what it's worth, I'm so sorry I have betrayed you.

As I looked up at Elle, a single tear rolled down her cheek as she replied, 'That's all I needed to hear, Ginny, that you love me,' She pulled me close and kissed me on the lips.

As I slowly made my way to my feet and embraced Elle, I whispered into her ear, shall we start again, 'Hi, I'm Ginny, also known as Sara. ' Elle laughed and said sarcastically, ' I know everything about you, Ginny and let's just say you may be even more surprised at how much we have in common, and from the bottom of my heart, I didn't expect that I would fall for you, so now that we are both here at this moment, let's just tell the truth, the whole truth and nothing but the truth and I'll go first'.

As I listened to Elle, she explained how she had been investigating her father since she had turned eighteen years old as she suspected he was not the perfect man and father she had thought he was. She had stumbled upon a plan to expose him through a private investigation into his links with terrorism. Elle had hired someone to see if he had been involved in her mother's death, and it had turned out her worst fears were true and that the person she had grown up to believe was her stepbrother was also involved.

She talked about how she had engaged with the assistance of some ex-British 'special forces' guys who were going to run a joint international operation to cover up the investigation by providing her with a security detail who could track her and her father's movements and find out the truth of his involvement in both terrorist activity and funding and the murder of her mother.

As she continued to speak, I tried to piece everything together without interrupting; so, had she orchestrated the whole operation from start to finish, how many of the team knew and were involved, did Ritchie know, and most of all, what the fuck do I do with all this?

I realised that Elle had stopped speaking, and I could see the sadness in her eyes that she did not want to be in this position herself; I could also see the deep hatred now she had realised and proved what her father was capable of.

There were so many things that I wanted to say at that moment, but the first thing that came out was, 'Why do you have a picture of Jane on that board?'

Elle explained that she had found the picture in a news article after researching me and making the connection we were a couple after she had been given information that her stepbrother had travelled to Afghanistan the same year that Jane was ambushed and killed; she had then found bank account details on her father making a substantial transaction to her stepbrother and what she assumed was a false charity medical clinic set up to finance the ambush.

I tried to hold it together, but everything came flooding back at once: the petty argument with Jane, taking her to the airport in a mood and losing her forever, my first meeting with Elle, our first kiss in the car, the first time we made love and then came the anger, for her father, he had caused all of this, he had brought us both to this moment, as I let out a cry that sounded like a mix of anger and pain, Elle held me tight. She whispered, 'Let it all out, Ginny, let it all out. We are in this together, and I want justice for Jane and justice for my mother, so let all that anger go, and with the love we have for each other, let's work together to bring revenge on that evil bastard who has never indeed been a father to me, he's going to pay for what he has done, trust me.

I felt that it was my turn to tell the truth. I began to tell Elle that I had recently found out about her investigation into her father and that I had received a concerning call from 'John' that we would have a briefing tonight about a family event. Before I could continue, Elle placed the palm of her hand on my cheek. She said, 'Ginny, I know everything, and I'm so sorry because as much as you may have been led into thinking I am being played, it's all part of the plan. As soon as I knew what my father was involved in and what he had taken from you, I knew we would be the perfect team to bring justice to him. To confirm, let me open the door so you can see how much you don't have to explain yourself to me.

I looked towards the wall I had entered through, expecting Elle to go to open it again. Still, she walked towards what looked like one of those food hatches you get in restaurants to send the food up and down; as she approached and pressed a button on what looked like a remote in her hand, the hatch opened, and there was Ritchie, I suddenly felt faint again.

'Ritchie, what the fuck is going on?' I shouted; I had never considered that he would be in this deep and be the person behind it all from Elle's side.

The sheer professionalism and seriousness of his tone threw me even more as he approached me and said, 'Ginny, I'm sorry, but this was the only way; I've been working with Elle undercover now, since a year after you lost Jane, I knew it was the only one thing in my life I could do for you to bring you inner peace truly and I couldn't resist but to get involved, and yes your right, it's been me all along leading this op, as the government won't do the dirty work as you know, but they are on board with this op, and they want Sharvani as much as we do and are fully supporting the op in the background, all the girls and guys have been specially chosen and are a mix of ex mil, Mi5 and Mi6. We are all here for one reason: to bring justice for Jane and Mrs. Sharvani.

At that moment, I didn't know whether to feel angry, sad, or happy as I was in total shock with everything

I had just learned in the past twenty minutes. I walked over to the whiteboard and stared at the picture of Jane, the one I had given to the newspaper of us both on holiday; she looked so happy. At that moment, as I stared at the picture, I could feel her staring deep into my eyes with that contagious smile, and I could hear her voice saying, 'Come on, get a grip, Ginny, this is all for you, get justice for me and live your life free of guilt'.

Elle placed a hand on my shoulder as she whispered, 'Jane was beautiful Ginny, you have excellent taste in women; look to the left and you will see my mother; she was beautiful too and I can hear her voice, telling me this is it, this is how we get justice together for us both, so we can move on and live our lives, and I'm hoping once all this is over it's me and you forever in the real world, no pretence, just love'.

As I regained myself and focused on Jane whilst taking in the love I could feel from Elle's voice and her hand on my shoulder, I finally got some words out: 'OK, I want nothing more, but what now, what's our next move?' I asked as I turned to look at both Elle and Ritchie.

Chapter 10 – In at the deep end

I had never seen Ritchie take on such a serious persona. In all the time we had grown up together, served, grieved, and argued, he had always brought humour, but now he was the most serious person in the room. His expression suddenly changed to one of concern. ' Ginny, I called you because I knew you would immediately go to Elle, and I needed to get you both together without causing any suspicion from Sharvani's protection team.

I need to be straight with this, and there is no easy way to explain it. Still, Maria has gone silent, we can't track her, her mobile phone is switched off, and we fear the worst, that your father has found out, Elle, that she has been investigating him; if he has her, there's a good chance he's going to interrogate her, and then everything will come out. So, we need to move quickly, as if he finds out you know he killed your mother, Elle, he's going to come for you, and Ginny, if he finds out about you and Jane, then this has all been for nothing, and both of your lives are in danger. Ritchie was calm, but you could hint at a sense of urgency, and I thought, 'What the fuck are we going to do.'

Elle interrupted calmly and collectedly, ' Ritchie, listen, if my father does have Maria, then I will be the one to find out. Don't rush to a conclusion or respond with anything just yet because that will send alarm bells to him more than anything; you know he has invited me round tonight for dinner and a big business announcement, right?' Ritchie looked perplexed. 'What? When did this happen? That's even more suspicious; you can't go, Elle; it could be part of his plan.'

Elle stopped Ritchie in his tracks. 'Listen, I know it sounds all very suspicious and adds fuel to the fire, but we have to carry on as usual, as hard as that may be. I need to attend tonight as I promise you I know my father better than anyone, and I will know for sure if he has Maria; if I go tonight, you make whatever backup plans you need to Ritchie, but everything has to go as planned tonight, and I need Ginny to be with me tonight as my father specifically mentioned to bring her along.

'For fucks sake Elle, this is a suicide; he's onto you both; why would he ask for Ginny to come along' 'because she's my protection, and my father likes her; stop being so paranoid, Ritchie, I promise you this will all work out the way we want it to, but we have to play this out tonight, for Maria's sake,' said Elle.

After finalising the arrangements for the night and not taking too much time, Ritchie left. I could tell he was anxious about how this was all going to play out, as I turned towards Elle to say that I should also return to the house as I needed to figure out everything that had just happened in the last thirty minutes and clear my head, she grabbed my hand in both of hers and said, 'Ginny, I need you to trust in me more than ever tonight, as this is how we get Maria back and most of all finally bring my father to justice. What I am about to say is just between you and me. I'm trusting you with everything I need to do this, and I need you by my side. I don't want any other justice for my father; I wish him to suffer like you and I have. I want him to watch his beloved son Omar, that rat of a supposed brother of mine who orchestrated my mother's and Jane's death, die in front of him and then suffer the heartache and loss we have, and tonight is my chance to do just that.

Let me get this right, Elle; you are saying you will kill your brother tonight? Right in front of your father, how will that end well? We will never get out alive. I asked. I'm not just going to jump up and stick a steak knife in his throat, as attractive as that sounds, Ginny, laughed Elle, 'I'm going to poison him so it looks like he's choked and watch my father's face as his beloved son suffers horrifically in front of him and there is nothing he can do.

I lied to Ritchie and Ginny; my father most definitely has Maria, and he knows about both of us, and he has tonight all planned to 'get rid' of us both, so we need to do this; I've planned it all, and this is the only way as he will be so focused on helping Omar, the plans he has for us will take a side step, and that's when we will make our move and call the team in. Then he gets brought to justice, rots in prison for the rest of his days, and loses his only true love, his son.

I knew this was a bad idea, but then I believed every word that Elle was saying, as I could see her love for me and her extreme hatred for her brother and father. This had to be the only way now; there was no other way out. If I didn't get on board with Elle's plan, it was very likely that we would both be joining Jane and Elle's mother tonight.

I pondered on that thought for a moment: Would it be so bad to put an end to all the sorrow and hurt and to be reunited with Jane? Elle, reunited with her mother? We would all be in a much better place and still all together. Again, Jane's voice was as loud as ever in my head, 'See through it all, Ginny. You will be with me again one day, but that day is not now; you need to do this.' I leant towards Elle and kissed her on the forehead as I said, 'Ok Elle, I'm in, I love you, let's fucking do this.

It felt like I had been gone for hours, but as I left Elle, I looked at my watch and had only been with

Elle and Ritchie for an hour. It suddenly dawned on me that I hadn't asked about Alana and where she fitted in; in all this, I went to turn around as I needed to know to ensure I didn't say anything I shouldn't, but there was no need because as I turned, there was Alana.

As I got back to my room, I sat on the edge of the bed and tried to take in what had unfolded in the last hour of my life; on the one hand, I felt betrayed by Ritchie and Elle, and then on the other I couldn't deny an element of relief, that I could now be Ginny with Elle and leave the facade of Sara. As I battled with my mind to try to get to some logical thinking, I realised that for once in my life, since losing Jane, something made sense; we had all been brought to this very moment to deliver justice, and I experienced one of those 'higher being' moments were upon I knew what I was about to engage in needed to be done and then maybe, just maybe I could get back some everyday life.

I had planned to pick Elle up at quarter to six, as her father's place was a thirty-minute drive, and he was expecting us at seven-thirty, which gave us an hour to discuss the plan. Elle had given me a burner phone and told me to only communicate through it and to leave my work phone in my room as it was likely that her father had a tracker on it, and we would play out a whole 'I've left my phone scenario when we got to Sharvani's'.

I put my phone in the bathroom and left it there to fit with the story, and as I left, I made my way to pick up Elle. I could not shake that stomach-churning feeling when I thought something would go wrong. I pulled up outside Elle's and straightaway noticed that one of Sharvani's personal protection officers' cars was parked outside; my heart was going one hundred miles per hour; we should have expected that Sharvani would ensure we didn't have an escape route, shit we had planned to stop and talk through the plan, I didn't even know what the plan was.

I parked the car as usual, not wanting to draw anything out of the ordinary. As I made my way up to the door, I was greeted by Alana, 'Hi Sara, Miss Sharvani's is in the lounge, and her father has sent transport for you, so you can relax tonight and enjoy your evening, Mr Sharvani has taken care of everything, she said as she smiled awkwardly and gestured for me to proceed into the lounge.

In the lounge, Elle was laughing with Zeus, who was Mr Sharvani's number one protection officer, and I watched for a second as he flirted with Elle. I wondered if he knew the plan for our planned demise at the hands of Sharvani. Still, I had always got on well with Zeus, and he seemed a genuinely nice guy, but he also appeared to be Elle's father's number-one confidant, or was he just another pawn on Sharvani's chessboard? As I approached them both I did my usual, 'Listen, Zeus, I know you're probably here so I can have a night off, but I'm getting paid to protect Miss Sharvani, not enjoy myself, and Zeus responded playfully, 'hey Sara, it's an order from Mr Sharvani and you know me, always obeying orders, let your hair down and have some fun and I didn't tell you this, but Mr Sharvani has got a real big surprise for you both tonight. I laughed along but glanced towards Elle, and as she glanced back at me and smiled, I knew we were both thinking the same thing. 'he's in for a big surprise, too.'

'Right, said Zeus, I'll go and get your chariot ready, ladies, whilst you ladies finish up here, and I'll meet you out front,' Thank you, Zeus,' responded Elle as she glanced towards me. I knew she was thinking the same as me, that Zeus mustn't know, as her father would have instructed him not to leave us alone for a second. Once Zeus had made his way out, Elle gestured for me to move through into the lounge; when we got there, she quickly went through a quick plan on using the burner phone in the back of the car to communicate to each other further on actions when we got to her father's house.

The churning in my stomach would not subside, and as I looked at Elle as she quickly talked through things, she paused, pulled me in close, kissed me passionately, and then pulled away and said, 'As tonight unfolds, Ginny, just trust me ok'. Before I could question what she meant, Alana walked in.

She said, 'Elle, everything is in place, be assured we have your back tonight, then glanced towards me and said, 'Yours too, Ginny' it has been so lovely to see you fall in love again' There was no time to say 'what the fuck Alana', I just accepted that like everyone else, she was much more aware of this whole situation before me. I just smiled and said, well, I guess we will catch up on that comment sometime soon.

As we made our way to the car, Elle glanced at me with that loving look. I just knew that everything that had happened so far in my life would be nothing compared to what would unfold tonight. I'd been through hell and back losing Jane, but this was my chance to break free from the guilt and longing to be back in her arms and finally make a fresh start with someone I truly loved. I had to take in this moment of just Elle and me before we embarked on the most exciting dinner date of my life.

Zeus took the usual route to Sharvani's, which eased my thoughts that he was not involved, as realistically and logically, he could have just taken us both somewhere remote and done the job there. I then thought that wouldn't be as rewarding for that evil prick Sharvani; his way would be to do it himself to ensure the job was done or at least send his sick bastard of a son to do it for him.

Through text on the burner phone, Elle reassured me all the way there, telling me to act as I would always when greeting her father, not to raise any suspicion and to follow her lead. Her calmness and control made her even more attractive than she was; she looked as breathtaking as always tonight, and I looked like Shane out of the L Word.

As we pulled into Mr Sharvani's estate, Elle sent me a final text, 'I love you Ginny, I'm only going to make you happy, I promise I will honour Jane's memory for you tonight, and I hope you can finally find peace and happiness and I want to be part of them both' followed with an emoji of a one-fingered salute. I laughed and thought, wow, she knows everything about me.

Chapter 11 – 'The Dinner Date'

Zeus pulled the car up at the front archway to the main house and said Right, you two lovely ladies, enjoy your evening, and I will see you later for the return trip home. 'Thanks, Zeus, you handsome fool,' joked Elle. Come on, Sara, I'm so excited to see what surprise my father has in store for us, as she flashed a flirty yet sarcastic glance my way.

193

As we walked up to the house, Zeus shouted,
Remember I said nothing, Mr Sharvani will have my
guts for supper, 'Oh, don't worry about that, Zeus,
he will be too busy cleaning up his son's whispered
Elle as she grabbed my hand as we walked up the
steps and into the lair of her father.

For a moment, I had forgotten that Elle had grabbed
my hand and thought shit, but as I pulled my hand
away before anybody saw, Elle looked at me and
said, go with it, Ginny, follow my lead as this is all
part of the plan.

I didn't know what to do then, but something inside
my mind kept saying trust her, Ginny. As we
approached the costly gold-plated front door, it
started to open. There stood Elle's brother, and
straightaway, he glanced towards our hands

interlocked and said, 'Oh Elle, tonight really, Father has one hell of a surprise for you both, and you're going to announce your sordid secret after all this time, remember I know everything about you little sister, he said menacingly. He looked at me and said, Maybe I now know a lot more about you, too, Ms. Rodgers. He smirked as he made his way outside and shouted, Don't worry, dear sister, I'll be back shortly to have dinner with you and in time for Father to reveal his surprise.

Before I could even think or feel anything in response, Elle let go of my hand and said softly, he's got no clue about what is in store for him tonight, and that's just sidetracked him for now, so relax and let's do this, my love.

At that moment, her father exited his quarters and bounded towards us. 'Oh, my beautiful daughter and

Ms Rodgers, don't you two look splendid tonight. Come on in. Let me get Alec to sort you some drinks, as he shouted for his porter Alec to go down into the wine cellar and get a bottle of his finest white wine.

I knew I had to keep calm and play this through, so as the ever-professional Sharvani had known for the past few months, I said quietly, Mr Sharvani, I am so honoured to be invited tonight, but I shouldn't drink as I'm here to look after your daughter. Before I could finish, Sharvani interrupted, 'Oh, Ms Rodgers, may I call you Sara? You are here tonight on my invite, and all security for my daughter is taken care of, so please enjoy yourself, as you may not get the opportunity again. he laughed, but I sensed a sinister twist in what he had just said.

As usual, I attempted again but was cut off and played along with my normal behaviours as instructed by Elle.

Sharvani's porter, Alec, came back into the lounge and directed us across to a solid marble table that was probably bigger than my home living room. It was neatly set for dinner, and Alec held out a chair for Elle. Then I was slightly relieved that we were sat next to each other. He poured us both a large glass of Sauvignon Blanc, and I couldn't help but wonder if it was spiked with anything as I took a sip.

I discretely scanned the room as Elle chatted away to Alec, who had been the porter since she was born, and I could tell she was trying to figure out if he was also in on whatever her father had planned. I couldn't imagine that he was, as he was a taciturn and caring type of guy who always looked at Elle with adornment. I started to think whether it had been sympathy and whether he had also carried the twisted secrets of Elle's mother's untimely demise.

Mr Sharvani came back into the room, and for a moment, I caught him looking at Elle with excitement and love and thought for a split second, what if he has no idea and this is actually some real surprise for his daughter and could he take his daughter's life away.

As my thoughts continued to wander, Elle gently said, Father, could I ask you to sit with us for a moment? I have something to tell you. As the words came out of Elle's mouth, I watched her father's expression change as she said, Father, I'm madly in love with Sara, and I would like your blessing as I don't want to hide it anymore.

I had not expected what came next from Sharvani, 'Oh my beautiful, beautiful Elle, I know all about this, and that's why I have brought you both here today; your wonderful mother always told me 'love is love' of course you have my blessing and I want to announce a surprise for you both at dinner with Omar present so I'll hold on to then, but trust me my darling I've known everything for a long time and I'm so happy we can clear everything up tonight and move forward, beamed Sharvani.

The whole situation was so uneasy for me. Still, I was fascinated at how calm and reserved Elle was. I sensed so much sarcasm in what Sharvani had just said, but Elle just played it back and played the doting daughter who had just gotten Daddy's blessing.

Sharvani's mobile rang, and his expression changed for a split moment, and then he glanced at us both and said, 'Ladies, please excuse me; I have some unexpected business to deal with; please be seated back in the lounge and pop open a bottle of my finest champagne as tonight we celebrate love, let's delay dinner until nineteen thirty, as your brother is traditionally running late'.

Elle stood up, moved towards her father, and kissed him on the cheek as she fixed his collar and said, Father, thank you for being so understanding; I love you; now deal with your business and hurry back as I can't wait to find out what our surprise is.

Elle had politely declined Alec's escort to the lounge and told him to go and have a well-deserved break. As she led me into the lounge, she glanced back at me; the look in her eyes was like the first moment she had told me she loved me, and for a moment, I was captivated by her stare. I asked myself why everything in my life came with such chaos; why couldn't this be me and her sharing our love and living our lives?

Elle turned towards me, pulled me in close and whispered into my ear, I've just slipped a bug under his collar, so we will know in the next half hour what his plan is for tonight. I love you, Ginny; please trust and stay with me on every move I make tonight. I promise you after tonight, there will be no more guilt or pain. It will be me; you are moving forward with our lives together. 'I love you too, Elle, I replied, lost in the moment and ignoring that this was the second time that tonight Elle had followed 'I love you,' with please trust me.

For the next hour, we drank very expensive champagne that I had never even heard of, and it was so expensive that the bottle that came in alone looked like it was worth more than the little place I called home. We giggled and chatted away, lost in each other until Elle said, 'Ginny, do you remember our first, let's say ', full encounter' down in the spa? Let's go and revisit. My father is going to be another hour yet, and we all know it won't take you long, she teased. My head was telling me, No, Ginny, come on, this isn't the time or place, but then my heart took over, and before I knew it, we were back where it all started in her father's jacuzzi, making love like it was our last night on earth, and for all, I knew it could very well be just that.

By the time we got back to the lounge and seated for dinner, it was almost eight o clock and Sharvani or

Omar still had not made an appearance; my paranoia was setting in, and suddenly, the fuzz of the wine and champagne I'd consumed so far subsided, and I suddenly felt sober. I could see slight chinks of anxiety in Elle. Still, it would only be me who noticed, as I could see the glint of love had momentarily disappeared from her eyes, now and again, and she would play with the clasp of her Cartier watch; then, as she noticed my glance, the glint would reappear, and she would smile so warmly. I just wanted to reach out and hold her to reassure her that everything would be okay, even though I wasn't so sure.

Alec came into the room and announced that Mr Sharvani and Omar were back and were just getting freshened up and would be with us shortly, 'Oh, tell them to hurry please, Alec, beamed Elle, 'I am just so excited to see what our surprise is.' 'All in good time, Ms Sharvani, All in good time, replied Alec, this time with a different tone to his voice. This is it, I thought to myself; this is where the night takes a turn for the worst.

Sharvani walked in with Omar in tow; he headed straight towards Elle and hugged her. he planted a fatherly kiss on each cheek as he apologised for his lateness and made up some lame excuse about Omar, requiring some fatherly guidance on settling business matters. He then embraced me and thanked me for my patience. It took every bone and muscle in my body not to contort from his hold. Still, I knew I could not show any negative body language, so it took all I had to play along as the doting girlfriend of his daughter, who had just been accepted into the family.

Omar, too, made towards his sister and embraced her gently, and I noticed as he kissed her cheek, he muttered something into her ear. Elle didn't respond to whatever he said. She just kissed her brother in return and said, 'Brother, do you always need a father to guide you in business' playfully but with enough sarcasm that would annoy the shit out of Omar, who loathed to be ridiculed in front of his father. 'Come on now, children, said Sharvani, 'let's play nice with each other and enjoy each other's company tonight as a family.

As dessert was served, I looked around the table and knew we were now closer than ever to Elle's plan. As we had eaten dinner, I was on edge, thinking at any time Omar would suddenly start to splutter and come to his untimely yet deserved death, but it hadn't happened, and I started to believe that Elle's plan had been foiled. I'd ensured that throughout the meal, I had only one glass of wine, which had been topped up by Alec just once, but I'd only sipped at it, conscious not to get too intoxicated. As my thoughts drifted, the muffled sound of an ongoing conversation suddenly started to become slightly louder but slurred, and as I looked towards Sharvani, he appeared to be slurring his words, and his expression had turned to one of menace; I looked towards Omar, who was glaring back at me but with a massive grin on his face, I then turned to look towards Elle, and as I momentarily caught her gaze I immediately tried to focus on her lips, as I tried to make sense of the impending darkness and fuzziness that was engulfing my head before the darkness came I managed to lip read, 'remember Ginny, trust me', then everything went dark and I slipped into unconsciousness.

Jane appeared as clear as ever; she was so beautiful, and her arms outstretched towards me as she said, Come to me, Ginny. Finally, you've found your way home. I shook my head, trying to clear the fuzziness and wanting to walk towards Jane, but my legs were heavy, and I couldn't lift them off the ground. It was like I was stuck in sinking sand; with every attempt to reach out and hold onto Jane, it seemed like I was sinking deeper. I looked towards the ground, and there, at the bottom of what seemed like a big black hole, was Elle, pulling onto my legs and saying, 'Trust me, Ginny, this isn't the end of us'. I felt like I was hallucinating, yet everything seemed so real; then all my thoughts crept into my mind, playing out loud my life so far and arguing about which step to take, towards Jane or Elle. What was happening to me?

Then suddenly, I was what seemed to be at the bottom of an ocean, swimming up towards the sky, holding onto every breath so that I could make it out of whatever situation I was in alive, as I finally made it to the top and broke through the water, I let out my breath, and as I shook my head to clear my thoughts, I realised I had regained consciousness. I looked down at my feet; they still felt heavy. As I shook my head, water beads flew out of my hair. I looked back down at my feet, trying to understand why they wouldn't move, and I figured out why they were tied to a chair. I was sitting on a chair, and as I gasped for breath one more time, I finally made sense of what was happening; I was tied to a chair on a sloping board with a cloth across my face and nose whilst water was being poured over my face, someone was waterboarding me.

Whoever it was suddenly stopped, and I heard a familiar voice say, 'Omar, that is enough; we need to get more out of her. I couldn't believe my ears; surely this wasn't happening. All this time, I had been led along a path of deceit. As the cloth was pulled off my face, I could smell her sweet perfume straight away, and as she knelt and looked into my eyes, I felt my heart rip out of my chest; how could I have been so fucking stupidly blinded, knelt in front of me looking deep into my eyes with that warm look of love was Elle.

Before I could gather myself or my thoughts to say anything, Elle placed one finger on my lips. She said, 'Ginny, we know everything about you, why you are here, what you have been planning all along, and now it's time to end it all. Make this easy for me, please. I apologise for the treatment my brother has shown you; I only left the room for 10 minutes. It's not our intention to make you suffer any more than you must; we need to know everything. As she gently kissed my forehead, those words came out of her mouth but with no sound, 'Please Ginny, trust and stay with me'.

Chapter 12 – 'Gamechanger'

Have you ever been sat watching a film and suddenly it ends, and you are like, 'No, it can't end like that.' Well, this is not that moment; I wish this were where the story ended, and I was blissfully reunited with Jane. I was not prepared for this moment to have the person I had fallen in love with rip my heart out of my chest with the ultimate betrayal.

All along, I was the one Elle had played; she had captivated me from day one. How hadn't I seen it? I fell far too quick; she told me her darkest truths in just five months; for fucks sake, Ginny, you are one hell of a mug; how have you fallen for all this.

As I played back in my head everything that had happened up until this moment, I tried to get a sense of where I was and if there was any way I was going to get out of this situation, but even if I did, how could I ever move on from this. I thought that I was just thinking everything through in my head, but as I heard myself say, 'Just fucking kill me, I'm done', I realised I had said it out loud and as I looked towards Elle, I repeated, 'just fucking kill me, you would be doing me a favour. Looking at her eyes, I could not understand why she still had that warm look of love and glint as she said, 'Ginny, we are not going to kill you; there are no murderers here,'. Elle knew what was coming next, and again, she knelt in front of me, placed a finger on my lips, and got close enough for me to lip-read, Please stay with me, trust me.

I remembered a book I'd read during my degree studies called The Chimp Paradox, and for whatever crazy reason, I remembered how to not allow the Chimp in me to respond and to hold on to my human. So with everything it took in that moment, I told myself to trust Elle and not to scream out, 'Trust you, your fucking brother killed your mother, supported by that evil bastard of a father, and you're saying there are no murderers here, what the actual fuck Elle.

I took a deep breath and said OK, what do you want to know, Elle? As Elle stood up and smiled at me

212

unknowingly to her brother and father, who watched on in the background, I prayed to myself that this was all part of a bigger plan orchestrated by Elle. It was Omar's turn to take charge of the situation, and as he walked towards me with that big smug smile, I just prayed that this was the plan and I would see this vile excuse of a man meet his destiny, Hell.

'So, you thought you would turn my beautiful sister into a dyke, Ginny or is it Sara? Laughed Omar. He knelt, and I could smell his tobacco breath as he laughed in my face and said, 'To be fair, my dear sister has put on a fantastic act and got you exactly where we need you. We know everything about you, Gina Brown, and your friend Ritchie or should I say stepbrother Richard Brown; you think all this time that you have been the ones in control; well, let me

213

tell you, no one in this land could outsmart a Sharvani, all we need now is the name of the person who is behind all of your plans, we had hoped to have your brother here too, you know like a big family reunion, but for now he's out of our reach. Still, we will catch up with him in time. So, for now, I will play a little game with you. You give us information, and we will provide you with something to resolve this situation.

I wanted nothing more than to spit in Omar's face as he had gotten close enough for me to do so, but I knew that wouldn't help me. I was intrigued to know what was going to turn the situation around for me; all the time Omar was speaking, I had noticed Elle in the background behind her father pouring some water into a cup, and I assumed it was going to be around two of waterboarding as she walked over with her arm outstretched to Omar to pass him the glass of water. Omar took a drink from the glass and said, thank you, sister, back to you. All you need to tell us is the name of the person running the show from your side.

I don't know what you think I know, other than I was here to look after Ms Sharvani, I replied. Omar tutted and looked towards his sister, 'Elle, how could you forget Ginny here? I think she's thirsty too, so please be hospitable and pass me a drink for her too, but she looks thirsty, so pass me that jug, and she's sweating, so that towel too, to mop her brow. Omar smirked as he looked back at me, and I knew it was time to practise those 'holding your breath techniques I learnt on special ops all those years ago, as this prick was about to waterboard me. I watched in horror as Elle, far too willingly, started to pour water into a jug; at that moment, I just didn't know what the fuck to believe was happening here, so I just closed my eyes and prayed that Ritchie would burst through the door at any moment with the team and end these fuckers once and for all.

As Elle walked towards her brother with a jug in one hand and a towel in the other, she had a look of concern on her face as she handed them both to her brother, 'Omar, are you ok, she asked'; I couldn't see Omar's face as he had turned away from me to take the jug from Elle, but what I did notice is that he had suddenly brought his hands up to his own throat and appeared to be holding it and slightly hunched over, he then suddenly fell to his knees, gasping for breath,

'Father, quick, cried Elle, pass me his water; I think he's choking, thinking Sharvani grabbed the glass of water and passed it to Elle, 'Here brother, drink this water; what's happening, Father, help him.'

screamed Elle, the penny dropped, this was Elle's

moment, she had put something in her brothers drink

as she had told me, this had all been an act and she

was playing out this scenario to get her ultimate

revenge.

Omar was foaming at the mouth, and the colour was

slowly draining from his face; Sharvani had knelt

beside him and was praying repeatedly for his

beloved son to be shown mercy by Allah,

Elle had moved across to the other side of the room,

unbeknown to her father, who was fixated on

helping his son. He didn't see what was coming next

as Omar took his last breath and fell silent; finally

meeting his maker, Sharvani slowly turned towards

where he thought his daughter Elle was standing, but

when he looked up, he didn't see his daughter

standing there, he looked up, and he saw me.

In my hand was a large piece of wood that Elle had given me after she had untied me, all of which had been oblivious to Sharvani as he had cradled his son, watching him take his last breath just as Elle had planned.

As I swung the piece of wood back before I brought it down on Sharvani's temple, Elle said, Dear Father, Omar was mistaken; you see, a Sharvani can outsmart a Sharvani. Ginny, don't hit him too hard, as he will live the rest of his life behind bars, mourning like we did the only person we truly loved.

As I brought the wood down on his temple, his eyes widened as he realised his daughter had been in charge of the game all along; as he slipped into unconsciousness, I could not help but smile as I recognised that look of heartbreak in his eyes just before they closed.

Every emotion that I had felt since the day I lost Jane hit me at once, and I just felt numb as I fell to my knees and cried like I had lost Jane all over again; at that moment, I didn't know what had overcome me, whether it was grief, relief, the joy of finally getting the revenge I had always wanted for Jane. Still, I sobbed like a child, and all the time I did, Elle held me in her arms so tightly I thought she would never let go. I felt despair, relief and longing all in that moment, and I just let it all out until nothing was left.

It felt like I had been there for hours kneeling on the floor leaning into Elle, but it was only a couple of minutes; as I regained myself and looked into Elle's eyes, she looked so sad as she said, Ginny, I'm so sorry I had to play it out this way, it was the only way not to spook my brother or father, please know that I would never have let you come to any harm and I drugged you so it wasn't down to my brother as he would have killed you. Please forgive me and know that this moment is all for you; I love you with everything I have.

But there is one thing that I need to tell you, and I think it will change everything for us. And please believe me when I only found this out this evening as we drove you here unconscious as Omar had blurted it out by mistake; it's Jane; after all these years, you have thought she was dead, she's not. She's alive!

I could not make any sense of what Elle had just

said, and I suppose at that moment I had cried all the

tears I had, so it was probably a normal reaction

after what I had just been through and then I heard

Elle say that I just responded with laughing. 'What

do you mean, Elle? Jane's alive, don't be stupid. She

was captured and killed; Omar must have been

sadistically winding you up to get your response. I

know Jane is dead; he's lying.

I thought that too, said Elle, but please watch this;

Elle passed me her phone, and a live stream video

was playing; it appeared to be from a head cam; it

was dark, and I couldn't see much, then the camera

was removed from whoever's head it was on, I was

so confused when the camera was then faced

towards its wearer was no other than Ritchie, 'what the fuck is going on Ritchie' where are you? I screamed, what is this shit about Jane being alive?

Ritchie looked stressed and like he was in the thick of it, 'I can't talk for long, Ginny, and I'm so sorry for everything you have been through and what I have had to keep from you and put you through, but we got some intel in the early hours of this morning that a British national was being held in Kunduz, and that she had been held captive for years to provide medical treatment to a cell in Kunduz, we've just extracted her Ginny and its Jane, she's here, she alive.

The camera flickered, and then another figure appeared in the darkness; she was wearing a hijab, but as she pulled it down and smiled as she raised her middle finger at the camera, it hit home that this was Jane, and after all these years, she was alive.

Virago – Game Changer

How can it be that one person could feel like they
had met their soulmate twice? After everything I had
been through grieving the loss of Jane, finding the
love of Elle, learning, and accepting that I could fall
in love again and feeling that after every challenge
thrown at me, I had come through it.

Yet, here I was, crashing back down to earth, trying
to pull myself together as I paced up and down
outside the hospital they had sent Jane to; I was just
minutes away from coming face to face with Jane
after four years of thinking she was dead.

Elle held my hand and pulled me close as she said,
Listen, Ginny, you know how I feel about you, and I
want you to know that I'm not going anywhere
unless you want me to. I know what Jane was to
you, and if you want me to give you some space or

223

spend time with Jane, that's fine; I will love you just as much as a friend if you wish to return to Jane. I get it.

Printed in Great Britain
by Amazon